Tales of My Time

vivienne.barker@gmail.com
All rights reserved
ISBN: 1523983647
ISBN-13: 978-1523983643

Revision 2.0
1st March 2017

Designed and edited by
Mike Smith
www.pcmike.uk

ACKNOWLEDGMENTS

My son, Michael, has had the drive, dedication and knowhow to turn a rambling pile of stories I wrote over some fifteen years, in France and in England, into this book, which I hope will live on when I am long gone. Until you start a project like this, you can have no idea just how much work is involved and I cannot thank you enough, Mike, for all you have done. Further thanks are due to Pat Bracegirdle who generously gave up her time to proof read this book.

I thank also, my friend, Patty Lafferty, who has also spent hours mentoring me as a writer. She is a wonderful person who continues to squeeze the best out of life despite cruel disability and she has taught me to look at my story-writing in a much more affective way.

A final thank you to all those people, family, friends, acquaintances, passers-by in the street who lit the spark of an idea at the bottom of these stories. A life without others would be a desert for me.

DEDICATION

These stories are dedicated to all the people whose paths crossed mine, who inspired me to write these stories and who will probably never read them.

THE STORIES

MOMENTO MORI

On Saturday evening, Ben and his mates, the brothers Albert and Arthur, were even more keen than usual to get started on their night out. After waiting for weeks, the fair had at last arrived and was camped just over the opposite side of the valley. So they took the short cut round the rim of the valley passing by the cemetery, laughing and fooling around on the way.

Ben would have been a bit of a dandy if he could have afforded to be. As it was he used to wear his father's long white silk scarf to go out on the town. It had become his trade-mark so to speak. It was always a winner with the girls who thought he was a dead ringer for James Dean.

'See down there,' Ben shouted, looking down into the cemetery, 'that family vault wit' angel on top? Me Uncle Stan's in there right now, as I speak!'.
'What for?'
'He's dead you clot. Died on Wednesday. They're going to seal it all up again after chapel tomorrow morning. I'm supposed to go but I

hate funerals and I never liked my uncle, any road up.'

'Why not?'

'Mean bugger 'e were. He and me auntie had the corner shop for fifty years and never gave owt free. Always sat like a monkey on his haunches in his chair by the fire. Never gave me as much as a toffee from his shop. Wouldn't give you the time o' day. No wonder they've got a damned great mausoleum.'

The evening was a humdinger! After a scrub in the tin bath to take off the coating of coal dust, the lads were ready for a few bevvies and a couple of games of darts at the club. At the working-men's club, they persuaded three of the girls to go to the fair with them. The lads thought they were the attraction, but the girls were, at first, more fascinated by the young woman in a glass case with nothing to wear but a grubby, leopard-print swimsuit and nothing for company but a coiled mess of snakes. They were repulsed yet attracted by the Siamese twin foetuses and other macabre abnormalities exhibited in glass jars. 'Well that's enough o' that,' said Ben, 'let's treat you ladies to candy floss and 'ave a bit o' fun on the walzters'.

Well, once on the walzters, they were practically on a promise. The girls squealed and threw themselves on the chests of the boys. Eileen clung to Ben and said he was her hero. It was a smashing night out which, sadly, ended all too soon. The three couples dawdled and canoodled towards home, along the top road, skirting the valley once more.

'Ben, what about a visit to see your uncle then? Show us what yer made of, eh Eileen?', Albert called out, winking at Ben's girl. 'Go on. You can do it! Do you remember jumping on that barge from th' canal bridge?'

'Yeah, I do - an' I fell into th'water and th'bargeman 'ad to hook me out an' all', admitted Ben.

'Go on', laughed Arthur, 'the drinks'll be on us if you do'.

Ben rose to the bait like a Jack Russell, 'Course - why not? I'll not need to go to the service tomorrow then, will I? I'll pay my respects tonight!'.

'You just go down there and tell him what yer think of him. He'll not give you an argument, will he?'

'How will we know you've done it though? I mean gone right into that tomb where he is?', asked Arthur.

Albert produced a Swiss Army knife, opened it up and announced, 'Our Fred got this from the body of a German soldier over in Normandy during the war'. He showed them every tool and blade, right down to the curved one for picking out the stones from horses' hooves. 'Ere! I'll lend yer this to stick in 'is coffin and we'll all come down in the morning to see. Go on. Get a move on. We'll wait for yer round the other side.' This was all to impress his girl of course, otherwise Albert would never have suggested lending his precious knife to Ben. And it certainly did the trick.

'See yer later alligator!', yelled Ben, grabbing the knife and heading off down the path. That white scarf of his was the last thing they saw disappearing into the gloom. Five seconds later and he was lost from view.

The farther down he got into the dense foliage the slower he ran, until he was walking, slithering, trying to make out the twists and turns of the path, catching his breath when a leafy branch of rhododendron slapped his cheek. The night air seemed heavy and he had to inhale through his mouth and nose at the same time. The odd hoot of a barn owl in the branches of a taller tree suddenly startled him.

It reminded him of the myna bird that Uncle Stan used to have in a cage near his chair. The thing that you never knew when you went through his shop was whether Uncle Stan was there or not, because the myna bird with its dead-pan 'Sithee wipe tha feet an put th'wood in th'ole!' could well be either of them. That was Uncle Stan's little joke. He could be master of his house without even being there. Ben and his brothers and sisters used to love tempting the bird with nuts and titbits.

Thinking of titbits, Ben stood stock still for a moment as a stabbing, guilty memory appeared from a lost place inside his head. He looked up to get his bearings by the light of a wispy, finger-nail of a moon. A huge predatory bird, with wings outstretched, was hovering not three feet above his head! Recoiling, heart stopping and beads of sweat pearling, he gritted his teeth and glanced again at the bird. The realisation that it was not a bird at all but the holy statue of Archangel Gabriel above the mausoleum, waiting to guide Uncle Stan to the gates of heaven, did nothing to reassure him. What did that inscription say? 'Vengeance is mine sayeth the Lord.'

A sob burst from his throat as Ben saw, in his mind's eye, Uncle Stan, standing in the doorway from the kitchen, catching him red-handed in the shop, with sweets bulging under his pullover. Ben's body was tensed as he waited for a 'lander'. Strangely, Uncle Stan looked at him gravely for a few seconds, bowed his head slightly, and then looked at him again, questioningly. Ben had been too cowardly to admit his crime, and the next thing Ben knew, Uncle Stan had gone back into the kitchen and closed the door quietly. Ben ran off with the booty and made himself scarce. Not a word had been mentioned about it ever since, but the guilt lingered on.

The door to the vault creaked when Ben touched it, and opened slowly to reveal a dank, black interior where an odour of perfumed oils barely masked the smell of decomposing flesh. All at once, Ben couldn't bear to be in the bosom of the afterlife and certainly not with the door closed. So he stuck his left foot against the door to hold it ajar and turned himself to the centre where the coffin must be. There it was. He felt the brass handle on the side, a little higher than he had reckoned. Adrenalin pumping, his breathing coming in short gasps, Ben leaned back to open the Swiss army knife with both hands. A cold draught of air flapped at the scarf around his neck. 'Damn! What the hell is that?'

He managed to twist forward and stab as hard as he could. 'O Lord, please don't let that coffin lid be off.' He felt the knife, the token of his bravery, stab into the wood of the coffin, just as he heard a sound like some material ripping. 'Thank God, I've done it. But has the knife ripped through that cloth wrapped round his body? Have I stabbed Uncle Stan? Surely I couldn't have. The knife's struck wood, not flesh. Never mind, the knife's stuck in all right.'

Fleetingly he thought of the adulation on his pals' faces when they found the knife embedded in the coffin-lid the next morning. Then he quickly shifted his weight to the other foot and kicked the door fully open. As he lunged through the doorway, his scarf tightened at his neck like a ratchet. Some unholy strength had him in its grasp. It was the hand of vengeance! 'It's sent to drag me to hell!' Clawing at his neck, retching from his throat, his hair prickling like thistles on his head, Ben wrenched and pulled at his scarf and at last, whatever power was holding him, let him go.

Eyes wild and heart thumping, he stumbled out of the tomb and scrambled straight up a bank, oblivious to thorns and branches, bumping into gravestones and turning over urns in his utter panic to be out of the cemetery. The need to survive totally overtook his mental state and he heard nothing, saw nothing, thought of nothing, save escaping from Hell. It was an eternity before he crashed into the wrought-iron gates at the far entrance, on to the road leading home. Ben burst onto the road - a wild apparition out of the darkness. The girls saw him first and their giggling trailed away to silence. They stared, their hands over their mouths, appalled at the shambling figure that was Ben.

Albert, a little ahead of the group, turned round and blurted out, 'Bloody 'ell, Ben. What's got into you?'. Ben gazed crazily from one to the other.

'Am I still 'ere? Thank God I'm still alive! Let's get going afore that thing in there comes after us!' He barged ahead of them, still stumbling. As they reached the first of the street lamps in the row of terraced houses, the light blazed unmercifully down on Ben's head after the gloom of the cemetery road.

The boys gasped. The girls screamed. They were staring at Ben's hair. His carefully brylcreemed quiff had turned a ghostly white - as white as his father's scarf hanging in tatters around his shoulders.

AUSTRALIA DAY

They could have been in any town hall in middle England. The mayor was trying too hard and the sandwiches and scones were curling-up on the side-tables in time-honoured fashion. Except that, outside, the sun was beating mercilessly down on the car park and everybody was in shorts - quite the opposite to middle England. Amanda stood rigidly in a dress and jacket noting, on the back of the programme, that the Australian national anthem was only introduced in 1984 (so no history there then). And there was the name of the place - Murwillumbah. Couldn't be mistaken for Middle Wallop, could it?

They were, in fact, in Australia for the first time to visit her husband's daughter and family. Of course it was a big adventure but her heart wasn't in it. She couldn't help resenting the cost of this far-flung trip. Besides, when people emigrate, they should remember whose choice it was. They could hardly expect everybody else to up-end their lives just to see them. Ah well, better make an effort to get on with them.

Amanda was convinced it was Kevin, the son-in-law's idea to come to Australia in the first place. Elaine would never have wanted to leave her family in England, but Kevin would. He had certainly fitted in within weeks of arriving the year before. Maybe it was his new-found Australian personality which made him so chavvy - even the way he spoke. Not, 'Would you like to sit down?', but, 'Put your bum down there'. You started complimenting his home-made muffins and the retort would be, 'They'll get you going all right, no question'.

It rubbed off on their girls as well. Right here, today, on this special occasion, the eight year-old was next to her, singing loud and confidently, 'Advance Australia Fair', her lips daubed with deep pink lipstick.

Amanda had to admit that Elaine, her step-daughter, seemed happy enough. Their jobs were going well and money wasn't a problem. One morning, despite the heat, they all went to the local market. 'Mom, can I have some of those cute little koalas? They clip onto your school bag. Everybody's got them. I really want some?' The girls had already adopted the accent and ended their statements on an up-turn, making it a question to which there is no answer apart from, 'Oh really?'.

Elaine suggested they look round a clothes store called Target. It was a cheap and cheerful store, to put it charitably. Elaine said the Australians pronounce it 'Tarjay' as though it were French. Was that supposed to make it sound more upmarket or something? Amanda was surprised to find a swimming costume that would actually do.

Right now the family looked delighted with their new citizenship. Amanda asked the girls what the best thing about Australia was, and Kaia said, 'Having assembly outside' and Sacha said, 'Having my own mobile phone', raising their voices at the end of both phrases as though they were asking questions. Then they said 'hoi' to some other little girls and shot off.

Elaine looked at her citizens' charter, then at Philip and Amanda. 'Dad, Amanda - we had to write out our wills when we applied for this. We've had to think about things very seriously. Like, if anything happened to us, who would look after the girls? There's friends and Kevin's parents of course - but we've decided we want them to come to you. How… how do you feel about that?' Her hazel eyes looked unusually vulnerable. Amanda wasn't expecting that. Wouldn't it be too hard for them with two lively girls whose language and interests they hardly understood? Wouldn't it shatter their well-earned retirement? Yet she knew Kevin's mother was a widow in her seventies. There was only one acceptable answer. Curiously, it pricked the backs of her eyes to say it out loud.

The next weekend found Philip and Amanda in Sydney, having a break from the family and giving the family a break from them. Sydney was a short, cheap flight away and pleasantly warm rather than steaming hot. The juxtaposition of the modern and the old was surprising. This was the history of Australia in one serving. She felt quite strange standing inside a two-up, two-down terraced house built in 1845 just like the one her grandparents had lived in, in the north of England.

On the first day back with the family, Kevin suggested getting up at 6am to walk down to the beach before the sun got up. It didn't seem such a silly idea since it was too hot to walk later in the day. So that's what Amanda started doing. Straight away she saw lots of people walking, jogging and cycling and nearly all of them greeted her with a 'G'dye'. To her surprise, they were quite polite as well as friendly, 'And they don't even know me', she thought. She tried saying 'Good morning', briskly, but when one chap said, 'Ooh, get you!' and winked, she thought it better to stick to 'Hello'. Well, what do you know - she'd just tried a 'G'dye' on a whim, and had a giggle to herself! Does shortening lots of words give you more time to do more surfboarding, running or cycling?

The girls looked cute in their school uniform of culottes, t-shirt and wide-brimmed hat. Elaine and Kevin asked Amanda to walk them down to the school next to the beach. They wanted her to hang around for the assembly. Other parents were there too. You'd never get that in England. It was all about welcoming new pupils to the school and making friends. 'Staat with a smarl ivrybidy!' You couldn't argue with that.

It was their last day. As she packed her new swimming costume she found herself saying 'Tarjay' instead of 'Target' and suddenly the irony hit her. She flopped onto the bed laughing.

As they said their goodbyes at the airport, Kevin gave Amanda a bear hug and she found herself telling him how good his cooking had been. The girls kissed them both and told their mum not to cry. Elaine gripped Amanda to her chest and sobbed in her ear, 'Please, please, come again'. Amanda's eyes watered. Philip kept his eyes on the floor. The passport man was looking again and they were propelled forward. They waved furiously then they disappeared.

Twenty-one hours later, two zombies were watching cases waltzing round a carousel. They recognized their cases just as they were beginning to wonder what you do if your cases don't come round. Were these cases really theirs? Of course they were. But what were these? Why, a little koala bear was clutching the handle on each of the cases.

BOXED IN

As the floor jolted the first beads of sweat trickled under my collar - my face a blurred patch of red in the mirror behind Alan's back. 'It's normal', I thought, 'after a dinner of foie gras, duck à l'orange and several bottles of St. Emilion grand cru'. Everyone else looked as panicky as me except Alan of course, our Head of Health and Safety. 'Don't worry. It can't fall. These things have automatic shoe-brakes that grab the ropes if it starts to drop. There's only ever been one that dropped all the way down.' It took some time for that information to drop too. Georgina surprised us before it did. 'For God's sake, press the emergency button!', she shrieked, the back of her hand smearing her vermilion lipstick.

Of all the stupid things to happen - just when I'd decided I was going to do it. The only reason I was in the lift at all was because of Georgina, the chairman's PA, whom I saw three times a year at board meetings and fantasised about at least 300 times a year (leaving aside the summer holidays with the kids and my annual skiing holiday with the guys).

Usually I take the stairs. I say it's the only exercise I get but, deep down, it's claustrophobia that's plagued me since my brother locked me in a cupboard for a joke.

Well, tonight was the night. The innuendos crescendoed, knees touching under the table, her making me taste the wine from the vermilion side of her glass, her hand over mine on the bread rolls. Margaret wouldn't have noticed a thing - such excitement is not on her radar.

I fingered the purple post-it with the room number on in my jacket pocket. It had had been folded minutely and threaded into my fingers as we were waiting in the lobby for the lift coming down. I had pretended it was just a glitch for as long as the wine's dulling haze lasted, but now our eyes were glued to the emergency light which flickered in response to Alan's pumping of the button - or was it my heartbeat?

'Maybe somebody'll hear us soon', muttered Margaret. Georgina screamed, her bosom heaving. I could only stare at her cleavage as the irony of being only two floors from her bedroom, to which I was going the next day after seeing Maggie home, forced a low, strangled laugh from my throat. I had taken a year to come to my decision and now the right of free will was taken away from me. I wasn't going anywhere.

'If it does drop, there'll be tons of steel cable under the cabin that'll coil itself so deep it'll cushion the impact.' Alan's face was finally drained now, as if he'd just discovered that knowledge wasn't power after all, and it takes Alan a long time to discover most things.
'Let's sit down and save our energy', said Margaret, folding up her coat and sitting on it, 'at least we're all relaxed after that delicious meal and the Bordeaux wine'.

'For Christ's sake', I thought, my eyes throwing daggers at the top of her head, 'it's all right for you with your regulation limit of two glasses'. I was stoking up for my adventure and right now my bladder was feeling the pressure. 'If they don't come quick…', I daren't let my imagination go any further.

We all slithered gingerly down - the two women with their backs to the mirrored wall and Alan and I with our backs to the doors, so I could see Maggie's straight brown bob in the mirror and for the first time noticed a top layer of grey hair, reminding me of a badger - don't they make shaving brushes with badger hair? Georgina's hair was bigger, blonder and bouncier. She was licking a stray lock of it and looking at me seductively when she suddenly stopped and said in a voice an octave higher than the sultry tones she used at my desk, 'But if it did, you know, drop, wouldn't it be a good idea to jump up just before it reached the bottom?'. She raised one buttock and stroked it.

Alan opened his mouth but I jumped straight in because any fool knows this one, 'You can't jump fast enough to cancel the rate of descent - you might as well lie flat on the floor'.

'Dead's dead', nodded Alan - his face like his words.

'Oh my God!', screeched Georgina, suddenly hiding her face on Maggie's shoulder, which was so not right that it made me cringe.

'Look, Alan, can you stand up next to me and help me prise the doors open a bit?'

I had strained my bladder for another half hour at least and was about to burst.

'You won't get out that way.'

'I know. I know. Just a call of nature.' We managed to pry open the doors just a couple of inches and I let off steam down the crack. Seeing it was so easy, and the women decent enough to start rummaging through their handbags, Alan followed suit.

We sat down again, taking all the time in the world and indeed it seemed that all the time in the world was gathering into this six by six-foot square box. The stillness dragged on. Maggie piped up, 'What make of lift is it, Alan? If it's an Otis, that's good news - they're the best'.

'No, it's not. It's a Schindler.'

'You mean it's Schindler's lift - like in the film?', I giggled nervously. 'I can't remember for the life of me whether it's good to be in it or not.' Nobody reacted.

Alan shuffled towards the corner of the cabin, accidently brushing Maggie's shoe - reminding me that I could still attempt to keep the channels of communication going between Georgina and me, only I needed to slow down my heartbeat first - my pulse was throbbing in my ears.

At some point, Georgina looked at me weirdly and opened her mouth. 'Dear God', I prayed, 'don't let her say anything. I need to play a cool hand, or the game is up, that's for sure'. She broke into sobs without taking her eyes off me. If only she would look at someone else. I thanked God that Maggie was too sensible to let her mind run amok and start imagining things that weren't true. I mean - nothing had happened - yet. My hands were clean.

An age later, Alan spoke. 'It doesn't take long for the in-lift etiquette to break down, does it?', he asked, looking at me.

'What do you mean?', I threw back, a little too defensively.

'Nothing personal. Just that everybody normally stands facing the front of the lift and here we are not two hours in, and we're sitting - men opposite the women, in each corner, and the two women close together. What does that say about us?' Before I could ask him if that was his idea of a joke, Maggie broke in.

'It means we all have our own way of dealing... what's that?', she exclaimed, as a banging was heard through the walls.

We all turned towards the noise which abruptly stopped and eventually, a deep, muffled voice came through. 'Anybody in there? Anybody there?'

Like a gaggle of squabbling swans we yelled, 'Yes! Yes! Help! Get us out of here'.

'We're doing our best', came the voice, 'the firemen will be here in a jiffy. They will have to move the lift down to the nearest door with the emergency mechanism'.

That jiffy lasted until dehydration set in - fear, alcohol, or time alone will do it anytime, let alone all three together.

'Whoever gave that bloke his health and safety certificate needs shooting', I thought, as a wave of nausea came up my throat. I managed to swallow it but knew it was only temporary. The thought occurred to me that vomiting might be a good result, considering the alternative. Georgina had stopped looking at me but was till sobbing. Maggie had her arm around her. Alan was next to Maggie, now on the back wall of the cabin.

'I'm ready for when they break in', he said.

'Do you have your mobile on you?', asked Maggie in my direction. 'You could ring the firemen to establish contact.'

'Oh, I thought you would want me to ring the kids to tell them not to worry.'

'I imagine that would have the opposite effect.'

'Anyway, I left it in our room. I didn't want the dinner interrupted.'

'Will you two SHUT UP!', yelled Georgina. 'We need to hear when they come back out there.'

'All right. All right. Keep your hair on...'

'...Or what's really yours of it', this bit to myself having spied the extension knots exposed by the mirror after she had squirmed about so much.

A long-forgotten jerk threw us all sideways - me into Alan's lap, Alan into Maggie's shoulder and Maggie nowhere, since she was hugging Georgina anyway. Alan put his hand on Maggie's arm and sat up again slowly, 'Well, if it doesn't happen - I mean if they can't get us out, I think we should discuss how we are going to survive as long as possible. Has anyone got any food? Or water? Ladies, if you need to pay a toilet visit, we men can stand and look into the corner'.

'Alan,' said Maggie softly, 'you are the only one to have thought of anyone else. Thank you'. We all fell quiet yet again, wondering if Maggie's words applied to us.

'I can't stand this!', screamed Georgina, rolling over and getting clumsily to her feet, 'I've got to get out of here!', and she started beating her fists on the doors, her hair straggling over her contorted face. 'And don't you start telling me what to do or not do!', she spat in my direction. Alan raised an eyebrow.

I couldn't react to Georgina any more. I was standing in my corner and the sides of the cabin were closing in on me. I had to push out my palms onto the two adjacent sides of the cabin just to keep them from compressing me. I no longer cared about the sweat trickling down my armpits and my chest. A worse trickle was running in my crotch too, unless I was imagining it.

My legs were beginning to buckle, so I slid back down to the floor, glad at least that the children were past their youthful ups and downs and settled now, thanks to Maggie's care. She had loved and kept us all together and always put us first. All in all, I reckoned, all this could have happened at a worse time.

'Come on, chap. Wake up. You're all right now. We've got you.' And so on, until my brain takes on board the fact that this is not the after-life, just the after-lift. I open my eyes to see Georgina stumble, kicking my legs in her hurry to get out. I don't blame her. You don't know what you've got till it's gone, as Joan Baez used to sing, but now I know what I've got.

And Maggie is standing, reaching down to take my hand. 'Let's go home straight away. I'll drive. I think we need our own bed tonight, don't you, love?'

BREAKFAST ON BOARD

'Why am I here? Why on earth did I do it?'

Susan stares at the napkin folded like a Roman blind on the plate in front of her. Should I unfold it and put it on my lap or will that begin to look ridiculous if the food doesn't arrive quickly? A large man three tables away tucks his napkin into his collar, American-style, like an overgrown baby in a bib, she thinks. She can imagine him banging his spoon in impatience. 'No, I'm not going to spread the napkin on my knees. I shall try to look as though I do this sort of thing every day.'

Susan has spent the last twenty years adapting to life on her own and to her clerical job in the civil service. She knows every form, with its reference number and its every application. She never makes decisions beyond her grade and is always pleasant and uncontroversial in the kitchenette where the staff eat their sandwiches. Her days and weeks have evolved into routines adapted to the avoidance of situations she can't handle. At first it was a sensible survival tactic, and has been so successful that there is no longer any conflict to be faced or decision to be made. She never steps out of her routine into the gulf of the unknown.

And yet, just now, she succumbed to an impulse. She has dived into the restaurant on Deck 9 of the cross-Channel ferry on a silly whim. Not that the ferry was a whim - far from it. She has been making the return journey for nine years now, to visit her brother and sister-in-law in Normandy. Turning into the restaurant was the whim. Now she doesn't know where to settle her glances.

'Hic! Bbbb hic!', a baby gurgles just behind her. Susan reacts before she can think and reaches down to the floor to retrieve the baby's dummy from under her chair.
'Oh, there it is!', smiles the baby's mother, taking the dummy from Susan's hand and putting it straight into her own mouth, then popping it back into the 'o' the waiting baby has mouthed. 'She's always throwing her dummy around. I'm sure she does it when she sees a lady like her granny. Thanks.' Susan would have loved to have been somebody's granny. If only…

She looks around at the insipid prints on the walls - muzak for the eyes. Looking out of the starboard picture windows has no attraction as the Channel is flat and featureless after leaving the Solent behind. It's nothing but a great yawning gap of sea to be survived before reaching terra firma. She begins to obsess about how she could look, as though eating in restaurants was a commonplace occurrence in her life. 'Look at that big fellow in the bib. He doesn't care a fig if anyone looks at him. I'd best do something whilst I'm deciding.'

Remembering the diary in her bag, she opens it on her napkin as a cover story. Hers is a diary of things to be done, not a sentimental record of remembrances past. That is why the next two weeks, her annual holiday from the tax office, are uninhabited. Staring at the two double blank pages, she feels an emptiness in the pit of her stomach that dismays her, like when she looks at the sea. 'Why do I not feel happy and excited at the thought of my holiday in France?' She has packed assiduously, taking all week to do it, choosing light but modest clothing with the correct accessories and sensible shoes for walking. She has interfaced each layer of clothes with tissue saved and re-ironed from last year. Even the packing list from the previous year was re-hashed. 'This is the ninth time I've done this journey to Normandy, to see Mathew and May. I've prepared everything down to the smallest detail. Surely nothing can go wrong now?'.

Suddenly, a wave of depression rolls over her. Maybe nothing will go wrong but that means everything on this holiday will be exactly the same.

She sees clearly that nothing can or will be different. Mathew and May will meet her at the ferry port in their matching jumpers. Every day they will have salad for lunch and May's pre-cooked casseroles for dinner. They will go for walks and carry flasks and sandwiches to avoid the unnecessary expense of eating out. On the Saturday halfway through her stay they will spend the morning looking around the local market then go home for their salad lunch. If it is warm enough they might eat lunch outside.

Feeling curiously imprisoned, when she should feel liberated by the empty pages, Susan shuts the diary and puts it in her bag. She wonders what you are supposed to look at if you are in a restaurant on your own. She hazards a glance over the tables. She manages to look at several couples and every time she does, she notices that if one of them lets their eyes stray from their partner's face, they look around at their ease. Of course, should they glance her way, they look straight through her as though she were invisible. 'It's easy for them. They have each other to talk to. They have no idea what it's like for me.' A person alone, thinks Susan bitterly, is cast adrift in a sea of faces without leave to appeal to any.

Usually, on the ferry out and back, she takes herself to the self-service, gets toast and jam and a cup of tea, sits only long enough to eat, then goes back to her cabin for the duration of the crossing and never looks out of the porthole.

It is true the waitress has been kind enough with her bland remarks, 'Il fait beau ce matin, n'est-ce pas? Vous voudriez du café ou du thé?'. Susan was happy to respond, but that seems a long time ago now, and Susan is floundering. Unexpectedly, as she braves a glance around the restaurant again, the large man with his napkin still tucked into his collar, catches her eye and smiles. Susan's mouth twitches at the corners in an automatic response but immediately she knows it's a mistake.

The waitress is back with the tea. 'Servez-vous avec des céréales et des toasts du buffet. Préférerez-vous du bacon et des œufs?'
'Erm. No. No thanks - just the buffet please.' Now, to add to her sufferings, she'll have to get up and cross the restaurant to help herself from the buffet. She hasn't prepared for that and has sat at a table miles away from the buffet. Any pleasure at her impulsive adventure has drained away.

As she makes her noiseless way across the room to the soft chink of cutlery on plates, her palms feel clammy and sweat beads on her forehead. 'Don't be ridiculous Susan! You're not walking the plank! It's only a restaurant on board a boat.' She picks up a bowl of cereal and a croissant, and walks the length of the table to get a plate. The all-seeing eye of the *Maître D.* makes Susan feel like an adolescent again.

Her father's solemn face atop his heavy chain of office looms into mind along with the usual back-kick of guilt she always feels when she thinks of his death and how she most likely provoked it.

Looking round to work out the best way back to her table she notices the big man again, just behind her. Without the napkin, she has to admit, he is well-made rather than simply fat, and he has an open, frank look. He is wearing the sort of ecru linen jacket which has a colonial whiff about it.

'Hello,' he says, 'delicious isn't it? I'm back for seconds, although I shouldn't - not with my figure'. Susan smiles wanly, and drops her eyes to her plate. His talking to her, the large man that is, has made her forget something she wanted at the buffet. That's the trouble - it's so tiring never letting your guard down. She hasn't slept well for years, since to do so would mean letting go, perchance to dream, sailing into the abyss of unchartered waters. If she did her father's face might loom up from the depths, dispensing judgment and dominating her horizon.

His face would be there, remonstrating, as he did when she had told her parents she was moving out into a flat now she was twenty. Her ears had rung with portents of doom. 'Why couldn't she live at home until she married?' She had gone nevertheless and she had been carefree - for a while.

Her mouth became dry confessing these things to herself - still marooned several paces away from the buffet table. Her carefreeness had ended the day after her first night of sweet, tentative lovemaking. How could she have known the young, handsome solicitor who drew up the lease for her flat was married? Before she knew the truth, a reporter from the regional newspaper was on her doorstep wanting to know if the daughter of the town's mayor had no misgivings about having an affair with a married man. The story ran for a week. Her father refused to see her ever again. Susan started to close in on herself lest it, or something even worse, should happen again if she ever dropped her guard. So she never had.

And now, because of this one, trivial, impulsive desire to have a proper breakfast on board the ferry, she is stranded in the middle of the restaurant, in the middle of the English Channel, not knowing why she has turned back to the buffet table, and with everyone no doubt wondering what this eccentric woman is doing.

'That's' it. Of course! I want a pot of hot water to make that awful strong builders' brew drinkable. Now where is the hot water boiler?' Her eyes run hurriedly and distractedly over the table. 'Ah yes, at the other end. Well of course, it would be.' Her hand grasps the pot at last and she turns to locate her table. Her other hand, balancing a tiny tray with the cereals and the croissant, is shaking enough to wobble the tray. She thrusts the hand holding the pot of water towards the tray, thinking to steady it. A stream of boiling water pours down onto her foot. She brings up her foot with a jerk and when the pain registers in her brain, waves of nausea overwhelm her. She wants nothing more than to pass out.

The *Maître D.* booms, 'Are you all right, Madame?' Never had she heard such inane words. It was as though the jets of pain had, at last, broken through the dam of her pent-up loneliness. She blurts out.

'How the hell do you think I am? I'm bloody hurt! I'm really hurting...' Her voice breaks into sobs. The nearby customers stop their chatting and chewing to stare. Soon all the restaurant's customers have become almost silent in their curiosity, not to say amusement, at this woman who has shouted at the *Maître D.*, and whose face is red and distorted with anger and tears, her foot hooked up behind her like a stork.

A protective hand takes her elbow. 'Let me take those.' Having taken the tray and the pot from her grasp, he guides her back to her table and sits her down, he kneels and starts to slip the sandal off her foot. Susan panics, recognising the big man, 'What... what are you doing?'.

'Trust me. I'm a doctor', he replies, looking at her with a wry but kindly smile. His light-hearted cliché has the effect of a life-jacket thrown to a person drowning. As he fetches some ice from the buffet and strokes it over her toes, Susan discovers she feels quite safe in the knowledge that this man has the best possible reason to be caressing her foot. His warm, dry palm holding, supporting, protecting her foot has her mesmerised, staring intensely at the back of his steel-grey head.

'How can anyone, most of all a stranger like this man, not be repulsed by somebody's foot, let alone mine?' But here is a man actually cradling her foot, as if he really thinks her incipient bunion is to be cherished rather than abhorred. His clean and faintly nutmeg smell reaches her nostrils. She wants to draw back her undesirable foot and lean closer to his aroma. How to stop this hardened shell of twenty years cracking to expose the soft and vulnerable centre still throbbing inside her?

'There you are. No unction these days for scalds, we just have to take the heat out of them.' He smiles again, his blue-green eyes under dark brows, crinkled with a kindly humour. 'It's a bugger having to eat on your own in public places isn't it? I normally hide behind my newspaper but I forgot to get one. Do you mind if I join you?'

DIRTY HARRY

I do my best to keep the house nice. A place for everything and everything in its place, that's what I say. I can't sit down until everything's neat and tidy - although it seems to get harder all the time. It's a shame to have to start the dinner really. It means messing up the kitchen again just to have something to eat.

The supermarket has such lovely dishes ready-made that I've started to cheat. Why dirty the kitchen when you can pop something into the microwave? Harry never notices - he'll eat anything I put in front of him. That way, I'm not back to square one cleaning the surfaces afterwards. You would think it's easy to keep things clean with new products coming on the market all the time, but sometimes I feel the bar is being raised just as I get up to the standard required. I have to try out all the new products just to keep up to scratch.

Last year a friend gave me a book which said you didn't need all these different products - all you need is vinegar. Well I did try. I used vinegar on the kitchen surfaces and diluted vinegar on the windows, the tiled floors and paintwork. It was very good on the taps and plugs to get rid of the lime scale but somehow it wasn't as satisfying as the cleaners made especially for the job they do. I like to see that they say 'antibiotic', or 'antiseptic' or best of all, 'kills 99% of all known germs'.

I've no time for myself, you know. Getting myself washed is more by accident whilst I spend time cleaning everything else like the shower, the bath, the surfaces and the toilet. It's Harry you see - he will leave his towel just thrown over the bath and his wet toothbrush dripping into the toothbrush mug. If I run my finger around the washbasin I can actually feel the grubby rim where the shaving water came up to - ugh!

We've been married nearly 15 years and it's taken all that time to get him to this stage. You should have seen how they used to live at their home. His mother used to taste the food she was cooking and put the spoon back in the pan! Thank God we've got fantastic products now to make it easier. There are antibacterial wipes for the kitchen that you throw away instead of a nasty germ-filled dishcloth and liquid soap. It seems unbelievable that people used to rub soap all over, and I mean all over their bodies, and then leave it for the next person!

Anyway, over the years I've managed to get Harry to realise how important a clean home is, but it hasn't been easy. I'm still trying to wean him off activity in the bedroom department. I used to put a towel underneath me but even that was just too - I just don't like thinking about it. I'd rather think about my house. My home is my life and I like to keep it squeaky clean.

I use the showers at the tennis club twice a week nowadays. It saves Sal a lot of work and me a lot of grief. To think I was so proud of marrying a girl who wanted to keep the house so spotless just for me. It's like she was pulling me up into a superior social position - and, to give her her due, she did. I was a plasterer on housing estates back then and now I sell thousands of pounds of computer equipment to taxi firms and I earn a bomb.

I just wish she'd relax a bit though. 'Having a clean house is essential,' she says, 'you never know who might come round'. But who comes round these days? The last time we'd people to a meal we did a fondue, so you can guess how long ago that was! I can't get into the house without taking my shoes off at the door. If I so much as venture into the kitchen I have to stop in the doorway until she's sprayed me with that infernal anti-bacterial spray.

She's never satisfied. There is always some microbe lurking somewhere. Last month she saw an ad on TV about how the handle on a liquid soap bottle can pass on germs. Her face dropped when she realised her lapse in perfection. They've apparently invented an automatic dispenser. You just hold your hand under the spout and hey presto, the stuff comes out on its own. Just how manic can you get?

Oh, I was proud years ago that our house was as clean as a new pin. As time went on though, friends who came to stay started to look nervous when she followed them into the bathroom and started spraying, wiping and folding the towels again. Come to think of it, nobody has slept over in, oh, 10 years.

A few weeks ago I did something I can hardly bring myself to admit. I'd taken my shoes off at the back door because she won't let me use the front one, and for once, I forgot to brush them and put them away. So imagine her face when she saw them. It's not that she shouts or screams or anything like that - it's just the look on her face - disgusted and somehow afraid. Is it me? Is that all she thinks of me? I used to come home and give her a kiss, but I bet any feller would stop if he kept seeing his wife wipe her mouth with a tissue afterwards.

So, anyway, the evening got off to the regular bad start and I admit I was in a foul mood by the time I'd had a wash upstairs (as per rules) and sat in the armchair waiting for her to serve up the meal. Then I felt a jagged piece of fingernail, so I pulled it off and was just about to get up and go to the kitchen bin with it when the phone rang. I stopped and saw her actually take a wet-wipe thingy from a box next to the phone and wipe the handset before she said, in her posh voice, 'Mrs. Harvey speaking'.

Suddenly, I felt an idiot pandering to her silly whims. What had I come to, following these trivial rules in my own home when I should feel exactly that - at home? Well, I slowly and carefully placed the fingernail bit on the coffee table, just in the space where the glass top meets the wooden edge, and you know what - I felt just like Marlon Brando or James Dean, except I was a rebel *with* a cause.

All evening I kept glancing at that fingernail, knowing she didn't know it was there and I got a kick out of doing it. It was a small victory for common sense, or the common man, or something, and every day that passed and it was still there, it lightened my mood. It was a little part of me she didn't know about and didn't clean up. Well, it was harmless enough, wasn't it?

You know, it's all very well men saying they like to be master in their own home but I know from experience that Harry appreciated being taught how to be clean. Cleanliness is next to godliness after all.

And the proof of the pudding is in the eating as they say. I've lately noticed him smiling now and then, so I know he appreciates his home and his wife and he wouldn't want things any other way. I am grateful to him for that. He is a dear really. I mean, a man can't feel things as deeply as we do, so I suppose I have to take him as he is - better the devil you know.

To think, a couple of years ago, I used to work part time as well as run the house, but in those days I didn't realise just how clean our house could be - should be. Yes, I should say 'should be' because if it had been clean enough - well, you never know, it might not have happened. Sorry, sorry, I don't want to go there. I have to stop thinking about it. Where's my list? It's Tuesday today, so it's upstairs - the guest bedroom and then the en-suite. Never put off till tomorrow what can be done today.

Thank God I do a lot of travelling in my job. Meeting people is what selling's all about and I find it's a real escape for me. In a strange way it's an antidote to the house and Sal - not that I'd ever leave - I couldn't live with myself if I did. Anyway, how could I justify that? How can you leave the perfect housewife? You know, that fingernail was there three days later and the very idea of its existence in the house tickled me pink. Come to think of it, maybe my mood is catching. One-night shortly after that, Sal and me actually laughed together at something on the telly.

I was thinking about it in the shower this morning and I laughed out loud. Well not too loud. I don't think she heard, but the laughing kind of tickled my bladder and I wanted to pee. Instead of getting out, putting a towel or two on the floor to get to the toilet without wetting the floor, I just thought 'sod it' and peed right there down the plug hole. I got another dirty little thrill from doing that - especially since there was no evidence left whatsoever. What the eye doesn't see, the mind doesn't grieve over. Exactly. And later that week - well, we actually got it together if you know what I mean. After all that time without my oats... I must be doing something right. Taking your courage into your hands always works, like it did after I got rid of everything after what happened. In one day I had that nursery repainted in white and a new bed installed. When she came back from hospital there was nothing to hurt her anymore and there is nothing to remind her now. Nothing she can blame herself for - you have to move on. These things are a mystery. My deepest hope is that I can make her happy again. I would love us to be a proper family, and, you know what? I'm convinced that her obsession with being uber-clean and germ-free is standing in the way. I'll just have to carry on with my one-man mission to introduce a little reality into our lives.

Last week, I think it was, I dropped a spot of mashed potato on the floor under the table and for one moment I hoped that she'd notice. She didn't - but could that mean I need to start being braver in my little peasant's revolt if I want her to get over what happened and move on? I mean what exactly could she do if I say, sneezed over the soup or picked my nose while I stirred her tea? It might upset her, but maybe that's what she needs after all this time. She wouldn't catch anything. No germs can exist in this house anyway. It's so damned antiseptic. What was it my mum used to say? You've got to eat a peck of dirt before you die?

The other day the bathroom was sparkling and clean, so I'd nearly done. You wouldn't credit the dust and the flies that gather in the guest bedroom. I don't know how the filthy creatures get in with all with the windows always shut but I do know they carry germs, sorry - microbes, and they have to be got rid of. This house had to be spotless if we were going to have any chance of, well, something wonderful happening.

I've got every cleaner and insecticide known to man. And yet, you know, you can't beat bleach. I know the environmentalists don't like it, but then they even like some germs, don't they? They talk about good and bad bacteria like on the telly ads. I saw one a few weeks ago saying their yoghurt had casei immunitas or something. But I don't believe it; a germ is a germ and bleach is the answer, especially now, if the doctor's right. I've had a few accidents and ruined some clothes with bleach, but my goodness it does the trick. I put it down the plugholes to clear any hairs or soap down there, on the surfaces and then I saw Harry's toothbrush mug. Ugh! It had some fizzy powder in - all dried on and crusty. Think of the germs there must have been! I had to put bleach in it - right up to the brim to get it all off. Then the back door went. He was home - and about time.

I told her I was sorry I was late. The traffic was deadly around Manchester. I was starving. I told her, 'I could eat a scabby donkey!'. I knew the sort of reply I'd get.

'What about me then?', she whinged. 'I don't just spend my time waiting for you to get home. You don't know the half of the work I have to do.' Blah, blah, blah.

'Okay. Okay, I know... well, I've got a treat for us. I've gone mad and bought a meal for two with a bottle of wine.' Then she said the wine might be a problem.

'A problem?' I was already looking for the corkscrew in the kitchen drawer.

'Maybe not,' she said, 'the doctor said just one glass of wine would be okay'.

I jumped and stared at her, open-mouthed, 'When did you see the doctor?'.

'I'll tell you', she laughed, 'but only when you've had a wash and cleaned your teeth. Leave your dirty clothes down here to go in the wash'. So I ran up the stairs two at a time in my pants and tried to swallow a couple of indigestion tablets, but I needed a cup of water to swallow them.

I couldn't help thinking how thoughtful Harry was, bringing home a meal for us. What would he be like when there were three of us? What would I be like? How would I manage to look after a baby and keep it safe from germs? Why should it be harder for me? My mum looked after me all right, and she had no husband after the war. At least I had a husband and a good one. I didn't want to lose him by being a nagging wife. I didn't want to lose him. And then it dawned on me… that cup of bleach in the bathroom.

I ran up those stairs and fell against the bathroom door. 'Harry, Harry! I love you! I love you! That cup! Don't drink it! It's… it's bleach! Oh my God!'

I sank onto the landing and sobbed. If God would save my Harry I promised myself I'd tell the doctor how I worry too much, how I've worried Harry too much and he doesn't deserve it. But I couldn't hear anything. I knocked on the door and put my ear to it. No! No! No! I couldn't bear it. I couldn't bear life without Harry. Then the handle turned and Harry peeped round the door.

'Where's that glass of wine then?', he smiled tenderly.

FROM FAR BACK

The man with his cap on at my kitchen table, his brogues shuffling under it, is my father. A faint whiff of pipe-tobacco, damp jacket and petrol meander over to where I'm standing - behind the kitchen counter. His piercing light-blue glance seeks mine, and mine keeps dropping down to floor level, despite myself.

His visits are now almost daily, and, to my utter bewilderment, I'm finding them hard to cope with. Yet this homely kitchen scene is what I have dreamt of for twenty-five years, for my mother broke off all relations with me that long ago.

As an ardent catholic, she disapproved of my divorce and simply cut off all contact. Over the years Dad turned up at the door four or five times, embarrassed and blustery. Yet what could he do? All he wanted was a peaceful home life, especially after he retired. It would have taken a lot of courage and shrewd diplomacy to stand up to my mother without disastrous results for his marriage. I can't blame him for taking the easy way out and going along with her wishes.

When, suddenly, my mother died, and I was again included in the family circle, I thought my dad and I would be able to pick up that close and loving relationship we had when I was young. My brother, Dad and I had great fun together (my mother usually looking after the home). Dad always had a child-like capacity to enjoy the simple and best things in life. He took us all over the Lancashire countryside, looking for birds' nests, tickling trout in the streams and exploring the pathways of Pendleside. He bought us far too many sweets and cheated us out of them when we played cards.

Once, in church, when the collecting-box was dangerously close, I realised my brother and I had no money to put in the collection, so I gave a dig to my brother, who poked mum, who gave dad a dig. He didn't miss a note of the hymn he was belting out in his fine tenor voice, whilst he leant forward and passed along the line of outstretched hands - a single salted peanut. My brother and I had sore stomachs holding in the giggles until the end of the service.

Well, obviously Dad too thought we would resume our old relationship because here he is in my kitchen. Only now I'm fifty years old and I can't seem to cross this bridge because so much water has flowed under it. He is acting as though nothing went wrong between us at all. He is cracking the same old jokes, clearing his throat before coming out with another opinion, spitting on both hands before buckling down to a job - even if it's only looking at the paper these days.

He doesn't elaborate much on what he is doing with his days - just a vague, 'doing my errands' or 'a run out in the Ribble Valley'. The trouble is - does he remember exactly where he's been? He doesn't seem to want to say exactly which villages he has been to that day, but it is always a 'lovely run'.

If only his pals from the bowling club or the old aunts he calls on would see sense and enjoy a drive out in the countryside with him, he could show them some beautiful sights, he says. He is more than willing to take folk out and, you would think, living on their own, they would appreciate it, but no, they've no get up and go, according to him. There's just old Sam Simmons who he takes out and about with him who appreciates the kindness. But, a funny do this, Sam has Dad's toolkit and won't give it back. It is always in his car ready for all eventualities and now it isn't. And who else has been in his car? Only Sam. Dad is going to have to take a look round Sam's house under some pretext next time he calls. He's not going make a palaver but Sam's not going to get away with it.

My great aunt telephones, her voice cracking with age and embarrassment, to tell me she is not going to get into Dad's car again. 'Albert's not safe to drive with', she says, 'and he's always coming round asking if he can take me out'. The last time he gave her a lift to the club she was terrified. She's very sorry, but can I have a word with him?

I tell myself it's not the sort of chat that would go down well from a daughter, so I talk to my brother about it. 'You don't have to tell me', Jack says. 'I've had a couple of people telling me about Dad driving absent-mindedly and having near-misses when he gives people lifts. Do you know he flung open his car-door outside Sam's house without looking and a car came past and took the door off? Before I could get in touch with the garage, they had given him a courtesy car, so he's driving around wondering where his toolkit is! I daren't go down to the bowling club. Apparently, he fell out with his team on trivial pursuits' night, stormed off and took somebody else's jacket off the hook and went home in it! What are we going to do with him?' We agree to get Dad to the doctor's somehow and maybe with the doctor there, we can get him to leave the car at home a bit and use a taxi.

Soon, the grapevine is buzzing with reports of Albert being seen in this or that pub, then in another and another until his inebriated state is becoming obvious. It's not that he is a heavy drinker, but he is forgetting how many pubs he calls at for a half-pint of mild, on his everlasting drives out. Old colleagues and friends are discreet. They honour past allegiances and rally round to take him home, delivering his car the next morning.

One day the telephone rings to say Dad is with the police after an accident in which he has breezed down a hill and careered into a line of parked cars. Thankfully, he is unscathed. We are very worried but when we talk to him it comes out angrily. Naturally, his reaction is one of dismissive indignation. He's been driving for fifty-five years, man and boy, and never had an accident before. How many accidents has he had, he'd like to know. Amazingly, the doctor has no power to stop him driving and neither have we. The police give him a choice. He must take a sort of driving test or surrender his license.

In a perverse way, I can't help admiring his pluck in choosing to do the test (the alternative is unthinkable), although I would dearly like him to stop driving. Would you believe it? He passes the test and immediately tells us off for 'getting too big for our boots'.

When I call round at his house, he doesn't object to me doing some tidying and cleaning as it's only natural a daughter should. I find carrier bags of food in varying stages of past sell-by dates or decay - in the sideboard, kitchen cupboards, hung behind the kitchen door and under the sink. He expresses genuine surprise when I present them to him. In his defence he tells me he is looking after the 'important jobs'. Why, only this morning a young man came round to offer to cement-rend the back of the house and the little yard. Grand chap. My dad has just written a cheque for £1400 to this grand chap.

Once or twice the police ring and say that a Mr Albert Starkey keeps reporting his car stolen. What apparently happens is that he parks his car in town, forgets where it is, but doesn't know that he has forgotten, so he goes to the police, reports his car stolen and then gets the bus home. Usually my brother is the hero who goes into town and treads the streets trying to guess where Dad has parked his car.

Our uncle, Dad's brother, rings to say Dad has a habit now of knocking at the door every two or three days to call on them. As it is getting a bit much for them, the last time - they were prepared. They had their pyjamas on! They told him that they had already gone up to bed, so, unless it was urgent... Dad's version is that his brother is going doolally going to bed at 7.30 pm.

I know that if we deprive Dad of his car he will be finished. He has never spent a whole day in the house in his entire life. That car has been his whole *raison d'être* since my mother died and without it, life would be a jail sentence. I am so torn between being sensible, and rooting for my dad.

One fateful day the hospital calls. Dad has been taken to accident and emergency, not to worry, relatively trivial injuries, but they are keeping him in overnight for observation. In hospital we get the story. He had left his car to go and look at the river in spate. His car had 'gone' when he returned, but no matter, he was only a couple of miles from home, so he 'jogged' down the road. Having tripped on a pavement and bleeding at the forehead, a couple from a nearby house had called an ambulance. Dad will have to stay in a medical ward until a geriatric psychiatrist can see him. That takes six weeks. Meanwhile he knows there is little physically wrong with him and keeping him there is purgatory for him and for us. This elderly man of seventy-four who has never worked inside for any length of time is now confined to a bed and a chair at the side of it.

He takes to ambling up and down the ward and the connecting foyer on a constant basis. The staff are getting slightly annoyed at him and visits are torture - not the being there but the trying to explain to him why he is there, and above all, the trying to leave when the visit ends. I tell him the sister wants to see me for a minute. This is a lie, as I don't go back to the ward. I tell myself it is only a white lie. Once or twice I actually push him back behind the doors to the ward and can't bear to look into his distressed and indignant eyes. He is beginning to wonder whose side I am on.

One evening Dad went AWOL. He had simply put a jacket over his pyjamas, slipped on his shoes and walked out of the hospital. He got a bus home and found no-one there (naturally), so he then walked two miles further to my uncle's house. My uncle and aunt had the shock of their lives when they opened the door. All Dad got for his courage and determination was a trip back to the hospital in an ambulance - and a diagnosis of senile dementia.

A month is then spent in a psychiatric ward, where my lying becomes habitual. I can't face any more of the barrage of questions about why he can't go home, or go out - they don't recommend any going out in case he won't go back in! The heartbreak of seeing him breaking down in tiny ways like wearing another patient's shoes or jumper is only relieved when he raises his eyes to the hills. Then he will reminisce about his youthful adventures, his job looking after the estate of the local squire and his love of the countryside. These moments are very precious.

When I come into the ward one morning, the sister and the doctor call me into a side office. I feel like I'm going into the headmaster's office at school. The evening before, Albert had tried the glass fire-door at the far end of the ward, then, finding it locked, he had taken the extinguisher from the wall and smashed the door in his bid for freedom. He had been restrained and brought back, having made it to the car-park. It is all too much like those films where everyone around the protagonist is trying to persuade him he is mad, but he fights valiantly knowing this is all wrong.

Eventually, Dad is found a place in a nursing home which can cope with him. There he tries hard to make sense of being in an old manor house with lots of tables in the dining-room. 'It's a nice place to stop off for tea', he says, 'but the coach will be setting off for the Lakes in a minute. I'll go and get your mother or else she'll miss it'.

Practically every day, with me trailing behind trying to take his mind off his objective, he will amble - no, shuffle now, from door to door, especially drawn to nice, solid ones with keys or latches, and try them all again and again. Or he will stare out of a window, identifying any bird which perches within view. He never really takes part in any of the bingo or even the sing-songs; surprising really because he has had a very passable tenor voice and has sung in church choirs (and pubs) all his life. It's as if he won't sing if he can't be free.

My brother takes him out for a walk but he is unexpectedly frightened by the noise of the traffic - Dad, who six months before was one of those car-drivers!

I cannot take in that a human being can shut down so relentlessly and so dramatically. Now, a year on, Dad is bed-ridden. His face is hollowed, his dark eyebrows and still dark hair stand out starkly against a pallid parchment skin stretched over his forehead, nose and cheeks. He lies on his side, knees pulled up gauntly under the thin sheet in a foetal position like a child with severe malnutrition. The utter despondency which I feel when I am carefully spooning some baby mush into his dribbling mouth is ineffable. When I look into his eyes, cloudy and lost, and whisper, 'Dad, it's Viv. Do you remember me?'. He struggles hard, his eyes searching my face in vain. 'From far back', he strains to whisper.

And that's it. No writing of memoirs in the twilight of his life, no opportunity to put things right for me or him, no feeling that I've been able to make things nice and comfortable at last. This is a death, the same death that all of us must face, but in this death there is very little dignity indeed, and for the nearest and dearest, no sweet closure, just a bottomless pit of guilt.

HELLO

Elizabeth stared at the ancient telephone her daughter was cradling in her hands and tried not to burst out laughing. 'You can't be serious, Lily!'

'Oh yes I am, Mum. It's so retro, it's cutting edge! I haven't used a landline for positively years! It'll look so cool. Where shall I put it? I do have wall socket things I suppose?'

'Of course you have, Lily, all landlines have. Makes me think though… back when we first got a phone, it was always put in the hall (or lobby as my mother called it). We had a new type of seat especially for it and I remember mother saying not to think we could spend longer on the phone just because we could sit down! Mind you, since everybody in the house could hear you, you weren't likely to spend a long time gossiping to your friends.'

'Yeah. Shame we all stopped using landlines years ago - except you and Dad of course. We've stopped wearing watches as well. We take our smart phones just everywhere. But there is something appealingly ironic about this heavy, old black thing with its twisty, threaded cord. Do you remember taking us to visit that grand old house where the décor was all Art Deco?'

'I do indeed, Eltham Palace it was, south of London - so stylish!'

'Well, the thing that sticks in my mind was the guide pointing out that the telephone was a new invention back in the twenties and that the owners were a bit wary of the new technology - apparently they thought people from outside could listen in to conversations in the room where the telephone was!'

Elizabeth chucked. 'Reminds me of how people thought the microwave cooked from the inside out and so you would cook your liver if you stood too near it! There's always some superstitions about new inventions, isn't there?'

'We don't need new inventions to be superstitious, Mum - there are still swivel-eyed loons believing in crop circles and UFOs no matter how many times we scientists disprove them.'

'And, even so, you are going to have this old-fashioned phone in your hallway? Now if I had one like this, you'd soon have something to say!'

'That's the whole thing, Mum. It's ironic. It's saying I know it's practically useless, but it's here to perform a decorative role - a romantic nod to the past.'

'It's more than a nod as far as I'm concerned. It takes me back to a time when I actually knew by heart the one or two numbers I regularly rang - there was no memory or anything to log your 'contacts' in. You know what? I couldn't tell you my mobile number to save my life but as soon as I saw that telephone, our very first telephone number at my mum and dad's, your grandparents' house, popped into my head. It was 42386.'

'Really? That's amazing! Maybe it made me think about Nanny's house when I saw this phone in the antique shop.'

'How to make you feel old, hey - when things you had around you when you were young, are called antiques!' They both laughed and Elizabeth suggested that her daughter should install the telephone (after a good polishing, naturally) on the little round table in the entrance to her flat, along with an arrangement of candles. 'It will be a nice conversation piece whenever your friends come round.'

Driving home, Elizabeth thought of the old terraced house and remembered the arrival of the first phone, the first on the street possibly. Certainly it had been an object of wonder on its special seat in the lobby. When it rang, which it rarely did, everyone rushed to pick it up and, for Elizabeth, even seeing the family name of Anderson in the telephone directory was awesome.

No sooner had she walked in the front door than Derek's voice called from the sitting-room, 'What's for supper, love?'.
'Liver and onions?', offered Elizabeth with a chuckle, still thinking of the sixties, 'My mother always made liver and onions on a Tuesday'.
'Well, I can't say I fancy that. Now, aren't you glad we can have a chicken curry because your husband is a 'new' man and is going to cook dinner for you? Anyway, don't play the poor little housewife card - you are a retired teacher with nothing to do but decide which cruise to book next!'
'You're right. I'm so lucky - and yet I think what a struggle it was to get on a course for mature students when I was thirty and had two children because my parents didn't think university was for the likes of us. It's always been my biggest regret that I didn't stay on at school. Nowadays nearly everyone goes to university. Mind you, it doesn't mean you automatically get a good job like back then.'
'Well let's be thankful our Lily's landed herself a good job', Derek smiled.
'I know. And a job she loves - interesting and challenging.'
'I'm very proud of her. Fancy - my daughter - a psychologist!'

Every time Elizabeth went to her daughter's flat and saw that old black telephone, it made her think of life in the early sixties with the newly-arrived telephone, The Beatles on the record player and those romantic comic magazines like Valentine that were all the rage with young girls her age.

One day, as Elizabeth set off to visit her daughter, she looked in the mirror as she always did before picking up her keys and opening the front door. She had to stifle a scream as she thought she saw her mother looking back at her in a headscarf tied over her hair. 'Are you okay, love?', shouted Derek from the kitchen.
'Yes, yes, love. I just trapped my finger in my keyring, that's all', she fibbed.

It took a few minutes driving before Elizabeth had calmed down enough to laugh at herself for tying her scarf round her head like women used to do in the sixties. Why had she done that? Was it that old-fashioned phone that had started a whole train of thought? When she arrived at Lily's, it was the first thing her eyes landed upon. She picked up the receiver and carefully untwisted the flex. Her middle finger sought the holes in the circular dial. It seemed so natural to flick the holes round clockwise and listen to the satisfying buzz as the dial returned to its central position. 'Careful Mum - it's connected now!', Lily shouted from her kitchen where she was making coffee.
'Oh, really! I didn't realise such an old phone could be connected. So, do you use it then?'
'Not really, but I love the loud double ring it makes when someone telephones here. It's just so British. Pity it's usually someone in a call centre trying to sell me insurance or offer me compensation for having been wrongly sold insurance! Anyway, my friends like it.'

Elizabeth was still holding the receiver when Lilly popped out to buy some coffee cartridges for her Nespresso machine. She put it down to pay a visit to the toilet. Adjusting her tights over her knees, Elizabeth found herself reaching around her hips for a suspender to hook a stocking on to. 'Good Lord, I'm going daft. It must be nearly fifty years since I wore stockings! What is going on in my head? It's that phone, it's really getting to me.' But she couldn't resist picking it up again.

Suddenly that number popped into her head again. 42386. She dialled it shakily. One continuous tone. Of course. How silly. She put the phone down. Phone numbers aren't that simple nowadays. More numbers ticker-taped across her mind. She dialled the same number again but this time she added an area code first. She caught her breath. There was the British double ring. Three times. Elizabeth struggled with her mind. What on earth was she doing? She told herself she would put the receiver down after five rings. She couldn't. Her heart leapt when a click signalled someone picking up. 'Hello, Burnley 42386,' said an eager young voice, 'who's speaking?'.

'I, er... my name's Elizabeth Barnett. Wh-who are you?' Her voice shook and her heart thumped in her chest.

'I'm Betty Anderson.' Elizabeth gasped.

'But, but... that was my name! My name before I got married!' Her hand shook uncontrollably. She sat down and stared at the phone.

'Who did you want to speak to? I'm afraid my mother isn't here.' Elizabeth went silent and then she heard sounds of a reverberating guitar in the background.

'Please, please me, oh yeah', sang some boys with a falsetto effect. Elizabeth put all her strength and concentration into her voice.

'S-sorry. Your mother is what?'

'She's out. She's gone on the bus into town.'

'Is that why you're playing pop records?', giggled Elizabeth nervously, then swallowed hard as tears blurred her vision.

'Sure,' the girl giggled in return, 'parents are so square when it comes to music. Oops, sorry - I suppose you're a parent yourself!'.

'Well, yes I am, but you're playing my sort of music. Will your mother be long?' Elizabeth's heart was pounding and she had to use all the self-control she learned when she was teaching.

'I don't think so. She's been out an hour. That must be long enough to look round the new Safeway supermarket. I hope she brings some cheesecake and yoghurt back. Have you tried some yet?'

'Er, yes. They're good aren't they? Just shows the Americans can be good at something!', said Elizabeth sarcastically whilst her head was spinning, trying to convince herself there was some rational explanation for this supernatural conversation.

'Sorry. I don't dig you. The Americans are good at just about everything from protecting us all from nuclear attack to I Love Lucy on the TV.' Turning away from the phone, the girl continued to another person, 'I think we'd better call it a day, Jean. You can take the Valentine magazines home. I've read them all. See you later'.

'Look, I'm sorry', she continued to Elizabeth, 'but could you ring back if you want to speak to my mother. She won't be long. I should be revising for my mock O Level exams - only two months to go'.

Elizabeth grasped the phone tightly, hoping not to make another boob but suddenly desperate to span the years. She had to eradicate the biggest regret she had ever had. 'D-don't go Betty. Just tell me one thing. Are you going to stay on at school to do A Levels? I-I hear you're a bright girl. It would be a shame to waste all that intelligence. And-and you could go on to university if you want to, you know.'

'Well, I'd like to, but I don't know. Mum wants me to get a nice office job. I suppose it will be good to have my own money - after I've paid my board, I mean. And I don't know anybody who goes to...'

A door banged in the background. Hurried footsteps and another door slamming. A different voice, low-pitched and breathless. 'Betty? Have you heard? President Kennedy's been shot. Shot in an open car with his wife sitting right next to him. They're taking him to the hospital in Dallas right now. For heaven's sake put the phone down and turn the television on!'

The continuous tone droned into Elizabeth's ear. She pressed the receiver to her ear as though she couldn't put it down. She was still pressing the receiver to her ear when Lily came back into the flat. Elizabeth tried in vain to explain. 'Oh Mum!', said Lily, 'What's the name for that psychological phenomenon? I know, it's the Braungoen Effect but you mustn't worry about it. Come on, I'll make us a cup of real coffee, hey?'.

'Actually, no. No thanks. Listen Lily, I want you to do something for me. I want you to ring that number again.'

'Now Mum, you know that it didn't really happen, don't you? You thought it happened, either because of stress, or even because you wanted it to happen. Let's leave it at that - like a very special dream. There's no harm in it, really there isn't.' Elizabeth threw Lily a desperate look and slowly and with deliberation, rang the number again. When she heard the double ringing tone, she held out the phone.

'Take it, Lily. I need you to listen.' Lily sighed. She reluctantly took the phone and tutted gently at her mother.

Suddenly, an eager young voice trilled out, 'Hello, Burnley 42386. Is that the lady who rang earlier?'. Lily dropped the phone as if it were a bomb.

The receiver swung under the table. 'Hello? Hello?'

HOW A KICK UP THE BACKSIDE CAN JUMPSTART YOUR CAREER

Here's a photo that tells a story. Let's see, there are roughly twenty people - all women except for three. There are balloons and mistletoe in the background, so it's the Christmas season and they are all waiting for the office party to start.

On the back row in the middle, arms spread-eagled round a girl on either side, is the boss. Mr Spencer, head of the Personnel and Wages Department. He must be standing on an upturned waste bin or something because he is a small man, dapper, suited, and with a small man's complex - you know, a bit too much of a swagger, like a bantam cock. He only smokes in his own office - not for fear of inconvenience to others, of course not, he's the boss, and besides, at least half of the department smokes. No, he only smokes alone in his office because he needs both hands free when out and about in his domain, spreading his particular sort of good will.

The only other two males are both boys really. Funny that - Mr Spencer, who must be well in his fifties, in no way regards them as sexual rivals because they are younger and better-looking, in the way that young women are seen as more attractive than older ones. That's because he's the boss - the most confident person in the scenario. He is king of all he surveys. His secretary works behind the glass partition in his little room looking out over all. If he has to squeeze past her on the way in and out of his room, it isn't his fault. If the wages clerks are all ladies and the head wages clerk is a lady too, it isn't his fault. One of the wages girls is even a winning beauty contestant - Miss Lancashire - and that isn't his fault either. So, in his domain, there is no competition.

One young man is James, in a suede waistcoat and jacket with leather buttons, looking out of the window (probably dreaming of his first car). He has already worked in Personnel for three years and has been told by Mr Spencer that he is not cut out for it. He is going to move to the Work Study department, responsible for timing the workers and thinking of more efficient ways of producing the goods. James showed me my duties when I started here a year ago, straight from school. It didn't take long as there is surprisingly little to do. At first I didn't mind the boredom as I was dreaming about James and not doing much myself. Not like the wages clerks, who have a weekly routine to get the wages done for over a thousand employees and whose machines only quieten down on Friday afternoons.

The day is cut into two distinct parts by the hour-long lunch, taken in the factory canteen. There is a partition between the workers' area and the office area, so that the workers don't see the tablecloths in the office area, the water jugs and the cutlery laid out - they have to make do with self-service, no waitresses for them. A large table in the office dining room is reserved for top management, amongst whom the Personnel Manager is proud to count himself. Under such apartheid, I can neither go into the workers' canteen nor sit at a management table.

I soon start to look around for escape from the boredom of filing and typing, which are usually done by lunchtime, unless I make so many mistakes that the carbon copy looks illegible. I find messages to take around the departments or perhaps charity money to be collected from the shop floor.

The wages clerks have no such excuses to leave their desks and merely observe everything through the glass partitions or strut to the ladies' room, patting their hair or circumnavigating Mr Spencer as he stands in the corridor waiting to stroke a passing body part. There is no escape if he goes directly to their desk and looks down their blouse. The head wages clerk looks at him severely, but with no effect. You can never be sure whether Linda, the beauty queen, plumps up her breasts as a treat for Mr Spencer, or whether it is a sign of her indignation as he leans way too far over her desk.

One day, Mr Spencer has a very large group of visitors to take on a visit round the factory and asks me to take half of them round. There are some questions I can't answer but I manage to ask the relevant foremen and all in all I find the experience most enjoyable. I even get to repeat the performance a few times. Mr Spencer doesn't ask James because he knows he is too shy and by now his interest is in Work Study.

The other boy, the one in the middle, is Edward, with a loud tie and a leery smile aimed at Mr Spencer. He only started a month ago. He is meant to replace James after Christmas. As it happens, I know Edward because he went to school with my brother. He has been put in an office of his own, next door to Mr Spencer and I'm feeling distinctly overlooked. You see, I have the foolish thought that I am being trained for higher things. It is soon only too apparent I am kidding myself - Edward is given the factory visits now and I am still filing and typing. Yet I know for sure he has only three O Levels. I wonder if I'm wasting my time going to night school, studying for A Levels. I am fast learning that school qualifications have no clout in industry, but obviously, gender does.

There is one woman missing on the photo. She's the one taking it - Edith. She probably insisted on taking it, come to think of it. She's the only woman who is completely off Mr Spencer's radar. She's near retiring and doesn't give a fig about impressing anybody, and so, when she's got through her paperwork at about two o'clock in the afternoon, she empties her overflowing ashtray into the bin and gets her knitting out. Nobody says anything. Mr Spencer's long past trying to make her life difficult.

Edith's lack of ambition gives her full play to develop her acerbic sense of humour. Right now, as she takes the photo for the umpteenth time with the beauty touching up her hair, Edward twisting round towards Mr Spencer who is guffawing and showing his brown-edged teeth, I can just hear her telling it like it is - as she coughs and splutters, the ash on her cigarette dangling dangerously. 'For gawd's sake, get your act together. Don't look at the boss, Edward, you need at least six years for promotion or a bombshell of a sister. Look at the camera. Linda, your hair couldn't be more bouffant if you had a balloon in it. Leave it out you lot, and say cheese!'

I'm there on the photo, on the end of the front row. I'm always pushed to the front because I'm only five feet two. Two years after starting work, I'm wearing my first suit with a straight skirt. I left after O Levels to get a good job in an office but I'm beginning to wonder what a good job is, and even more, what an interesting job is.

Edith gets the photo Mr Spencer wanted for the company magazine and we all look relieved and move away to get ready for the party after work. The wages clerks scurry back to their desks to finish the payroll for the week; James pretends to be engrossed in a flow-chart on his desk; Edward looks at his watch and pretends to look busy picking up the phone and dialling. I pretend to be busy filing pension cards and Edith doesn't pretend to do anything - just lights a fag and leans back in her chair, watching the rest of us pretending.

So then I hear Mr Spencer come out of his office and head towards the wages office. I shuffle in towards the filing cabinets to make ample room for him passing and glance up to catch James giving me a shy smile from his desk. 'Oopsa-daisy then!', cackles Mr Spencer into my ear, as he pushes himself into my back and casually fondles my right buttock with his free hand. I inhale his greasy breath and my ear flinches at his oily tones. I let out a screech.

The comptometers shudder to a halt. The wages girls stare. My first instinct is to look across at James again but he doesn't know where to put his red face. Edith stabs her cigarette out and shakes a fist at the boss' back. The wages clerks shuffle. I spin round to see the boss turning away - whistling as he does so. My reaction is visceral. I swing back my right leg and kick him sharply up the backside. It is a vicious kick, full of anger for myself and for James' humiliation.

Mr Spencer, stunned, turns round to face me again, rubbing his buttock. 'You'll pay for this! You mark my words, you'll pay all right!' His spittle hits my eye. We both stand rooted to the spot for a second then he turns his enraged face away and bolts out of the department, wrenching open the weighted door. The wages girls clap hesitatingly, then the machines start up their clatter once more. The beauty stands up, sashays over, looking me up and down and says, 'Well done, Jan. Somebody needed to do it. But watch your back. He'll be after his revenge now'.

I decide not to wait for retribution. I go to the General Manager upstairs (where we only go for interviews) and tell him. The general manager is above the petty goings-on of the offices and the factory and concerned only with the yearly results. He always nods politely when we pass him in a corridor and shakes hands at the Christmas party. 'Is there any real injury, er, Janet? You must realise that Mr Spencer has been personnel manager here for twenty-one years. You are very young, you know. If you keep your head down, it will probably be all forgotten by the holidays.'

When I am splashing my face in the washroom, Edith heaves her body in the door and gives me a hug. I dodge the ciggy stuck to her lip as best I can. 'You done well, gal, but like the beauty said, he won't forget it. This place isn't for you anyway. I see you restless and bored with what you're doing. Even James is only a distraction. You look around for something else.' I begin to realise it's all over for me. If I stay, he will make my life a misery. I wonder if all office jobs are the same.

When I get home my Dad says he'll go and sort that Mr Spencer out, but Mum wonders if I have got above my station, questioning the regime. It is Friday and the local paper has arrived which always gets Dad's attention. 'Hey, there's an ad here for the government. They need people to train as teachers', he calls out, during the adverts on the black and white telly. 'Fancy, you can get a grant of £2000 a year! Maybe your night school classes will come in after all. You don't have to go away to university - it's at a college in Chorley. You can get there on the bus.'
'As long as you don't have to go away...', Mum trails off.

And that is how, four years later and thanks to Mr Spencer's bottom, I am a fully-fledged teacher. And here's the photo - Edith gave it to me saying she didn't want any mementoes of forty years' forced labour. Look, there he is - Mr Spencer, with his arms around the wages girls, looking like the cat that got the cream.

KINDRED SPIRITS

Since my retirement from the local primary school two years ago, my days have been unremarkable and devoid of surprise or impetuous moments. I have even come to think that a little of the combative stress of the classroom might be better than this comfortable but oh-so-boring routine.

From the moment Barry brings up my morning tea with the newspaper, to the nightly patting-on of anti-wrinkle cream, there occurs nothing to set the pulse racing. I long to be led astray in the manner of all would-be heroines, strike out off the beaten track, discover the real me. What I really do however, is the cleaning and cooking necessary for two retired people, a tidy couple of moderate habits who have been following the same daily routine for at least thirty years.

True, twice a week I go into town whilst Barry works at keeping his handicap below 17. I do the shops of course, otherwise what could I talk about to the girls at lunch afterwards? But, to tell the truth, filling the house with twigs, dried petals, swags and bows ceases to be exciting after three decades of the same - ditto for clothes-buying. When you have filled all the built-in wardrobes in all three bedrooms, you do lose track of the clothes you have. I sometimes wake up in a sweat wondering what to wear.

These days, when it's my day at the Oxfam shop, I leave the ladies' stuff to the others and pick out the best of the gentlemen's clothing for Barry - he is so laid back about clothes that, left to himself he would always be in baggy corduroy.

'Don't judge a book by its cover', he says, 'l'habit ne fait pas le moine'. He does this to annoy me sometimes – he quotes in French just because he was a secondary school teacher. He reads Maupassant on holiday. I'm more of a Maeve Binchy woman.

In the evenings, I find I have edged into the category of the 'bodice ripper' reader. A harmless escape surely, if I am to accept that my adventures in real life are over? Barry is usually upstairs, in the box-room - sorry, study, playing bridge on the computer with Omar Sharif. Granted, my husband has never given me a lot of trouble. He's been very undemanding all our married life (well, somebody has to be responsible for not bringing unwanted children into the world - God knows, I've taught enough of them).

So right from the start, we decided not to have children in order to enjoy our hard-gained middleclass comforts. We have never regretted our decision although we have always found it a good idea to go abroad for Christmas. When you are in Fuerteventura or Mykonos, you don't feel the absence of family at all. Nobody comes around to warble carols through the front letterbox and you don't feel that pathetic sadness at opening presents from each other and nobody else. Furthermore, our home has always been a haven of peace and tranquillity - no noisy, ruined children or those aggressively monosyllabic teenagers.

I'm sure our very occasional love-making, perfunctory and sometimes downright painful without extra help to lubricate the moment as it were, takes place mostly to justify the queen-sized bed (bought circa 1985 along with the total-look fitted wardrobes).

Anyhow, paperback love stories that I pick up from the Oxfam shop when I'm doing my stint, do give me a bit of a fantasy rush. When I'm reading, the heroine is me. The tall handsome stranger falls for me and despite other women getting in the way, he comes to claim me for his own at the end. Of course, I know it's only a dream world but don't we all want to escape from a humdrum life some of the time?

Once a week, there's one page in The Newbury Times that delays my getting up for an extra half-hour or so. It isn't the births, marriages, or even (despite a lot of the entries being too close for comfort) the deaths columns that I scrutinise, or the pathetic flotsam and jetsam of life for sale in the classified. No, it's the Kindred Spirits page - a whole page of lonely hearts looking for their dream partner.

Those entries which are on the lines of 'successful fifty-something male looking for slim adventurous female for fun, frolics and more' make me incandescent because the chap in question is obviously not mentioning his paunch whilst being arrogant enough to order a slim lady (personally, I have always been a more comfortable build), and I admit that I am cynical enough to deduce that the chap in reality, plays bowls and has an artificial hip.

That particular Friday, in the Letters Only section which is redolent with the sort of old-fashioned romance you can't find in the voice-box column, there was this:

An ordinary guy, in the prime of his life but trapped in a marriage without passion, seeks a woman in a similar situation to share tender moments. Absolute discretion is assured and required in return.

It was a thunderbolt. My hands tingled like they do when I have a near miss whilst driving the car. No doubt about it, cupid had hit his predestined target. From that moment, I was propelled from the mattress, through the shower and into my navy-blue ex-teacher's outfit.

The morning spun by, entirely spent in the stationery store. You see, I had to have just the right paper (maybe parchment?) with matching lined envelope. No matter how passionate my words, they would never come out right on the office paper from David's printer which we use when we complain about things (which I insist we do on principle, otherwise the country will go to the dogs).

My friends remarked on the colour in my cheeks and my refusal to order the usual large meringue, but I was ready for them and quoted the '5:2 intermittent fast diet' as the culprit. They were so intrigued by this latest way to truth and light that their attention was easily diverted. I was not going to give this game away. It was mine and mine alone. 'Absolute discretion.' That was the way forward if I intended to go ahead and seize the moment. Although I honestly think the moment had seized me. I had no choice in the matter at all.

The following morning I was up before my tea arrived and had to plead the need to vacuum the house early because the ladies from my charity were calling round for morning coffee. This had the effect of ejecting Barry into the garden leaving me to write out carefully what I had spent all night preparing in my head:

Dear Guy,

Your entry in the Kindred Spirits column went straight to my heart. How I empathise with what you are going through! And how I know I can answer your needs. Any relationship we embark upon will, of necessity, be limited to moments snatched for ourselves alone, in order that we may continue our separate routines with some semblance of sanity. Be that as it may, I am ready to embrace love again in the re-assuring bond of mutual discretion. Please let me know how you would like to proceed.

Not being able to trust the Royal Mail and being altogether caught up in the clandestine thrill of it all, I rushed into town the following Tuesday, wearing a sort of practice outfit with patterned tights and a skirt almost up to my knees - just in case. It would also serve to acclimatise my entourage with the new me which was emerging as a result of my *affaire de cœur.*

I went straight into the local newspaper office and asked the girl on reception what would happen to my letter. She was a nice enough girl but wholly unconcerned with the urgency of the situation. I suppose she had decades of opportunities to come - unlike some of us. She proffered the information that all correspondence was forwarded to the box holder on a weekly basis, and that she would give me a number. I accepted gracefully and walked briskly home thinking about the delights life was about to offer me if only I exercised patience.

Ten days and four visits to the newspaper office went by before the girl at reception deigned to pass me an envelope. Even then, I had to endure an hour with Wendy and June before I could rush home to my quiet kitchen (mind you, their comments on my looking trim and younger were pleasing, if somewhat belated). His reply contained precise instructions:

Could you be in the railway station buffet next Tuesday at 11 am? If you are sitting at a table in the window and reading The Newbury Times, I shall know who you are as I pass the window. I shall be wearing a yellow tie.

The day approached. I seemed to have a hundred things to do. I looked out clothes I hadn't got into for years. I went to a hairdresser new to me as my regular one would have coiffed me as usual for a wrinklies' charity lunch.

Tuesday came. It was windy and raining heavily. Up and in the kitchen early in my dressing-gown, having had to sit up half the night to preserve my hair-do, I was wondering whether to take an umbrella or wear a hat and itching to see whether Barry would leave for golf at all on such a morning. Oh why couldn't he just get out of the way? At last he appeared in his car-coat announcing that the newspaper hadn't been delivered. He didn't comment on my hair, but then he never did. He went off at last to the newsagent's and thence to meet his golfing partners.

Having parked the car in the railway car-park and run back to a shop to buy a local paper, it was one minute after eleven when I fell through the station café door, wiped the steam from my glasses and saw that, thank goodness, a window table was free.

By the time the waitress had brought a mug of tea and I had shaken out the newspaper, taken off my hat and arranged my reflection in the window, it was ten past and the train for Oxford was arriving at the station. Who should come in at that very moment but Wendy! I hid myself behind the newspaper, my nerves completely on edge and then, thank goodness, I remembered her vanity. She never wears her glasses apart from when driving and so, when she gazed round the café as she asked for something at the counter, I knew her pale blue eyes couldn't see beyond the pile of muffins. I was safe from tittle-tattle.

But drat it! I had just missed a man who was now walking away down the platform and looking back disappointedly before turning to board the train. He was getting into the first-class carriage. It had to be him.

It was too late. I had failed to seize my chance of love. Tears began to prick the back of my eyes so I hid behind The Newbury Times again. No sooner had I done so, when someone slid gently onto the bench opposite me. I sniffed as quietly as I could, coughed and practiced a coquettish little smile as I started to look round the edge of the newspaper. A hand was smoothing a bright yellow tie over a manly chest. My eyes travelled upwards and I saw the face I have lived with and slept beside for thirty years. The smile faded from his face.

'Oh my God', he whispered, as if I wasn't there.

O SOLE MIO

It's grand this time of year. I went for a walk this morning round Primrose Wood and over to Hambledon Moor. Now, where's the newspaper? Where have I put my glasses?

The food's good here, I've no complaints. It's not the same though, being here without Janey. Still, good food and me behind the wheel on an open road, that'll do me. Janey's never minded me going off for a drive in the country, or calling in on family of a Sunday morning after church.

It's all very nice and that, here, but I'm an outdoor man, me. Mind you, I've done my time down the pit. That's what you call real work - crawling along the tunnel for hours at a time. I used to sing sometimes down there and let the echo resound through the caves. My mates used to laugh at me. 'Alf,' they'd say, 'what the hell is there to sing about down here?'.

And I'd sing, 'O Sole Mio'. And they'd clap if they could hear. Sometimes they'd shout through, 'Give us a bit of Violetta, Alf!', and I'd sing, 'Hear my song, Violetta. Hear my song, beneath the moon'.

I was so glad to get out. After that, I could never work inside again. Then I fell lucky, working for the local landowner as his estate man, repairing farm buildings over the whole of the Burnley to the Todmorden area. Sir Edward and his wife lived in a grand house outside a village. We had a tied cottage an' all, but my wife couldn't settle. She felt taken advantage of when she was asked to cut the children's hair, or do some cleaning, because nobody offered to pay her.

Edward - I only call him Sir to his face - would get on the wind-up telephone from the big house and ask me to come up and cut the lawn. No matter when, Sunday morning, Saturday tea - it was all the same to him. We did like to be asked up to the big house at Christmas for Midnight Mass and that, but Janey didn't like being taken for granted, so we went back to town.

Our Louise said her mum's dead! Passed away three years ago. Nay, she's pulling my leg. Janey can't have died! Why, she's never had anything wrong with her.

Ridiculous. Barmy. First Louise said her mother's dead and I know for a fact Janey was here this morning. And anyway, anybody can trip over a flagstone. I know I shouldn't have been running down the road, but I was just anxious to get back home, when I realised somebody must have stolen my car, that's all. So, why have they kept me here so long? There's no point in hanging around any longer. Ah, now, I've lost 'em again -where did I put my car keys?

Don't know why Louise is worried about me. What the blazes for? It was only a bump on the head when I fell on Rossendale Road, I just need to get my head down for a bit of shut-eye and I'll be all right...

What a carry-on over a trip over a flagstone! I've walked miles over the moors before now, tracking down water pipes that were broken, digging it all out and replacing broken ones, single-handed with nothing but a spade and a bag of tools. I don't know why our Louise keeps fussing.

Some of these farmers up on the moors live in the past, you know. Up over Bacup, there's a farm where a brother lives with his two sisters. The sisters never go out - only the brother goes to market and fetches the necessities and the like. These sisters - you've never seen anything like it - long black skirts, aprons and bonnets. They feed the chickens and keep house. They all talk a lingo you can barely understand... ee, let me get out onto those moors again. I can't stand being penned in like this much longer.

I've left that hotel. No good to me. All I did was lie around all day. Here's the town centre - keep going - Rosegrove ahead. Our little two up, two down has been my home ever since I married Janey. Owning your own house - grand. Janey's marvellous at managing the money. She always puts food on the table. I never have to worry about a thing. I hand over my wages and she gives me a bit back for my baccy, running the van and putting a bet on the horses.

Ee, I'm worn out. Thank God I'm home. It's getting dark. Now where are my keys? For Christ's sake! And the car? Where is it?

Hello! Hello! Janey?

I don't believe it. I've left my keys somewhere. She'll never hear me. Okay, don't panic. I'll go on up to my brother Jim's. Up Padiham Road. Mustn't strain myself. Remember your angina, Alf. Blasted cars. They're so inconsiderate these days, drivers. Don't you pip your horn at me, you idiot! I've been driving fifty years, man and boy and I've never done that. I'm a knight of the road, me… okay, where's Jim's house? Oo, I wish I didn't feel so worn out…

———————————✦✦✦———————————

What sort of hotel is this, then? It's no better than the last. My daughter tells me I've been here three months. I told her not to be stupid. I can't have been here three months. I've only been here two minutes. I only put a bet on a horse running in the St Leger, this morning! 'Smiler' it's called I think - or was that one running last week?

What do I want to sit down and have a talk for? Sitting. Bloody sitting. I want to be off over t'moors out there! I told Louise, 'Do you know what them hills are, them you can see over there, lass?' Of course she didn't. Brought up soft, the young lot are. Don't go anywhere without a car. Well I damn well know every one of them hills. I used to go up there tickling trout in the rivers when I was nobut a lad.

Once, we were up there, tickling trout in a stream. This posh chap strolled up to us. He stopped and said, 'I don't know why you bother here, boys. You won't get anything'.
I looked up at him and said, 'Well, mister. You just watch'. 'Cos I'd seen a big 'un, just hovering there. And I leant into the water and just lightly tickled it under the belly till it stopped dead. I grabbed it and

threw it up on to the bank and while it was wriggling away there, I just said to the posh bloke, 'Will that do you, Sir?'.

Louise told me I have to give her my washing. Washing? I don't have any washing! Janey does the washing every Monday without fail. She sees I have a clean shirt, vest and underpants every day. Whose are these pyjamas? They can't be mine, I don't wear pyjamas.

Louise said such a terrible thing. It can't be true. Janey isn't dead. What a thing to say! How can she be dead? We've never had a night apart from each other. Here's her photo. She's so beautiful. I was very lucky to get her. There were other fellows after her at the Empress when I saw her. Ee, I am lucky. Well, it's time to be off home now. My car's just in the car-park.

That fellow in the white coat says I can't drive my car! Nay, bugger it all. I've been driving a vehicle for more years than he's lived, and never been had for speeding. All right, all right, I suppose I could cut down on the driving a bit.

And who says I can't look after myself? How dare they? What do they bloody well want me to do? Who are they anyway, to tell me what to do? Louise says I'm rude about them but she needs to get real. I eat what I want, when I want. Isn't that good enough? My wife has scrimped and saved all our lives and I don't bloody well know what for. I want to take her on more holidays - but it's not happening. We could have gone to Italy again. She loves Italy - well, we both do.

By the left, what a figure I cut in that little tavern in Sorrento! They were all singing, like they do, and they started to shout, 'Hey you English! You sing something?'. Well, I sang 'O Sole Mio' from beginning to end, in Italian, mind... and their eyes popped out of their heads. 'How you know Italy songs?', they said.

Well, I started again, 'Sul mare luccico, lastro d'argento...'. They went mad they did, clapping and whistling. That brought all the old songs back to me that I learned from the Italians in the pit. So I gave it all I had. They loved it!

What the hell am I here for anyway? Why do they keep coming when nobody's here and poke and prod me with some sort of tests? Well I'm as fit as a butcher's dog. And I want to go home. So they can bugger off and boss somebody else around.

Why is the damned door locked again? Who are those people? Just because they're wearing white, they think they're always right. I've got to get out. That fire extinguisher will do it. Just break the pane and I can open the door from the outside.

And it's summer and I'm outside again where I belong. The thrushes don't mind that I took their eggs many moons ago. The hawthorn is in blossom at the bottom of the lane. You can see the tracks leading up to the farms on Hambledon hill as clear as lines on a road map - white, chalky lines winding ever upwards. The farmer's wife will welcome me with some snap when I get up there. She's only too pleased to have some company, you know. It must be hard for these folks to be isolated, penned in you might say, with the continual round of milking, feeding, getting the silage in. They don't get many visitors.

Where is he, farmer Jack? It's nearly seven in the morning, and he usually picks me up to help with the milking before I get off to school. He only gives me the odd bob or two, but it's enough for me. I might go on the football match on Saturday, see Burnley doing their stuff. Or I might set off to Blackpool next weekend on my bike. At any rate, I don't mind. It gets me out of the house for when my dad gets home. He'll be plastered as usual. He won't bother where I am. As long as I'm out of the way. Crickey! He's a long time coming, Jack is. I'll set off anyway. He'll see me on the way up.

Blackbirds, magpies, the smell of the factory chimneys way down there. I can hear Uncle Bob's pigs grunting in his allotment, the stream trickling down the path - no time to fish for tiddlers, the cows won't wait. This is my idea of heaven, this is...

'O Sole Mio...'

ONE WOMAN'S GREED

A young woman boards the ferry at Harwich, England, leaving for the Hook of Holland. She constantly looks down at the bundle in her arms as she negotiates her way past the foyer and down the passage to the lounge. There she breathes a sigh of relief and collapses into a reclining seat. Her face lights up at the smile the baby unstintingly gives her and she tickles his cheek where the smile has dimpled it. They gaze into each other's eyes for a while, the baby's eyelids droop and he is soon asleep. The young woman leans back her head to doze. A tap on her shoulder jolts her wide awake.

Vanessa was an only child born into a middle-class, home-counties family. Not that life was to be handed to her on a plate. That was not the way her father thought at all. She must show true grit and rise to the top, even if his money had put her half-way up the ladder to begin with. 'Preston! What sort of university is that!', he barked on hearing where Vanessa had got a place, 'It must be a doddle to get a first there!'.

Looking at the unkempt, council-house types around her on the campus, Vanessa secretly agreed but worried constantly about her coursework. Whatever was lacking in originality of thought was made up for in abundance by the illustrations and expensive presentation. Her 'Art in Marketing' tutor complimented her and treated her to scones in a teashop in the town. 'Your presentation is impressive, Vanessa. With a couple of sessions of one-on-one brainstorming you should be able to come up with some really good stuff', he said, picking a hair off her cashmere coat. This was like candy to a baby, and Vanessa saw rather more of the tutor than his portfolio. In fact, it took so long to come up with some really good work that by the time that happened, Vanessa was coming up with her breakfast.

The chivalrous tutor disappeared on an Erasmus exchange for two months and the next time Vanessa saw him on the campus, his interested look of amused playfulness had been replaced by a world-weary expression and a wife and child at his side.

Despite her father's mutterings about gunshots and lecherous lecturers, family money paid for an expensive abortion clinic in Berkshire and Vanessa vowed she would never lose control of her life again.

The 2:1 degree was, in the circumstances, very acceptable to both her father and the Versailles College (which also accepted her father's money of course). This offered Vanessa an MBA course which was known to springboard young aspirants up the corporate ladder.

Magda loved her schooldays in the little village of Paklow in Poland. She felt privileged staying on until sixteen when most young people left at 15. Her father, a miner like most men in the village, would have liked her to go up to Krakow to study at the university but she was needed at home with her mother being ill.

Her father did the best he could. He was determined she would not dull her bright mind on the assembly lines, nor break her back in the fields. He went to speak to the fathers at the seminary nearby which had been revived these last few years thanks to the influence of Karol Wojtyla, the great pope.

Working at the seminary was an honour to a staunch catholic family like Magda's and she knew it. She also began to learn English as it was used amongst the seminarists who came from numerous countries. They taught her how to tune a radio into the BBC World Service and there were English newspapers around for reading during her breaks.

Magda continued her life, enjoying her mundane but genteel job, escaping into the study of English and helping at home now that her mother had given up her cleaning job at the school. Everyone knew that the cause of her mother's depression went back some years, but nobody could do anything about it, least of all Magda.

Yet Magda's heart had broken too, when her little baby brother had died. It was she who had found his little 18 month old body in its yellow baby suit, curled up in his cot. There had been no illness beforehand. The investigating doctor discovered little teeth marks on his cot and deduced it was death caused by lead poisoning.

Her mother had keened and wailed for months, then, one day, picked up her cleaning bucket and started back at work. Magda wasn't allowed to grieve so openly, it wasn't her right to do so. As children do, when they have little opportunity to talk to someone, Magda blamed herself for her little brother's death. Wasn't she the one who always put him down for his nap? Didn't she sometimes leave him a bit longer than she should, just to finish a puzzle, or do some homework?

———————✦✦✦———————

A leading perfume house in Paris took on the young Vanessa and groomed her for the top. Vanessa never put a foot wrong in her career from that moment on and climbed the corporate ladder with only a little stepping on others on the way. By the time she was thirty-two, Vanessa was Head of Marketing and based back in London. She thought she would look for a husband at this point, because her daydreams were running beyond the smart luxurious flat she lived in, to a grand house in Kensington. This time Vanessa would be in control and love would have very little to do with it. What she wanted was a fortyish ex-public school-boy from an 'old' family, who would have his own money and interests and be fairly biddable at home.

Tim filled the bill admirably and never gave so much as an opinion over Vanessa's planning of a sumptuous but tasteful wedding in Mayfair, followed by a cruise around Malaysia on Sea Cloud Two.

Life continued beautifully for another six years, until Vanessa admitted to herself that Tim's company was less than riveting. She could, and did of course, holiday with girlfriends and choose the most exotic business trips to make, but even so, she wondered whether a child wouldn't be more amusing. There was a little hitch here. She had stopped using any form of birth control but nothing was happening in the baby way. IVF treatment was sought in Harley Street and, after the third attempt, Vanessa was pregnant with twins. Vanessa had done it again - gone one better by having two babies at once for maximum efficiency and minimum body droop, and what was more, there was a boy and a girl. A perfect result!

Of course there was no question of festering at home for Vanessa, she wanted to be back in the buzz of the office as quickly as possible. Tim did not demur, remarking only that after just three months, she was as svelte and glamorous as before. Vanessa put an advert in a London magazine for a nanny. Being an excellent judge of character herself, Vanessa eschewed the agencies and did her own interviewing.

A career was not for Magda but she had a pleasant enough job at the seminary. Some of the students would speak to her in English when they found out she was interested, as some of them were homesick, and, truth to tell, some of them needed the softness of a woman's conversation. They even included her in their Saturday evening television viewings, when they watched English TV programmes as a relaxation.

One young student, training for the priesthood, always left 'The Catholic Herald' on the library chair for Magda. He took to mentioning an occasional item from the newspaper in passing the time of day. 'Did you read about the Muslims? They are having an international discussion on how to pray facing east when you are travelling in Space! Ridiculous isn't it?'
Magda laughed politely and replied, 'Yes, it's angels on pinheads again, isn't it?'. Once, in handing her the newspaper, their hands brushed softly, the young man's eyes looked straight into hers and glistened with supplication. Magda dropped her glance and blushed.

Some two weeks later, Father Superior called her once more to his office. There was, he said, no duty sadder than the one he must do today. Priests were, she must know, a rare commodity in our modern world. He could not afford to lose any from the seminary, the church was in dire need. He had to tell her she must leave the seminary. She was too much of a temptation to these young unformed priests who must toughen themselves for a life of chastity. He was sure she would understand and he would help her with a small grant of money. What could she see herself doing?

What indeed? What could she possibly do? She had no job, and would have no reputation when the gossip spread through the village. Although her mother needed her, she also felt an unspoken reproach for her little brother's death whenever her mother looked at her. She glanced at The Catholic Herald on the desk. 'Help me get to England, Father.'

When Magda walked in, having turned her straight skirt around so that it didn't look 'seated' at the back, she had left behind her a job washing dishes in a greasy spoon in Peckham, but had brought with her a reference from the Father Superior in the seminary near Paklow, written in impeccable English. 'Why do you want this job?', enquired Vanessa.

'I think I need to care for people, like I did my little brother in Poland and of course, the priests in the seminary.' Magda looked steadily at Vanessa from under her earnest eyebrows. Vanessa knew she could trust this young woman.

Tim and all the family congratulated Vanessa on her shrewd choice. The young woman was modest in her dress and behaviour and she certainly knew how to look after babies. They sank into contented sleep at her rocking and she could interpret every squeak they made.

Magda felt the responsibility of these two tiny creatures very keenly.

She slept next to their nursery and thought of little else but them. Indeed, after feeding, bathing and changing routines, there was little time left except for a walk around the park, pushing the twin buggy. This was the highlight of Magda's day. Passers-by, those not rushing straight through the park as a short cut, might peep into the buggy and coo with admiration for the two little blond, curly heads. So well had Magda bonded with the children, that she was the one to put them to bed at 7pm even when Vanessa was home. Vanessa absolved herself by telling Tim it would be upsetting their routine if she interfered.

Guy and Daisy blossomed in Magda's care. Their little limbs uncurled and kicked with pleasure at bath time. As their tiny mouths found and suckled on the bottle, their pupils gazed at her and dilated with instant gratification. Although it was out of fashion, Magda used baby powder to dust their bottoms at nappy changes. She told herself it was still better than cream, but knew also that the nostalgic smell revisited memories of her Mikal.

It was hard work indeed with two armfuls of baby to keep happy, but Magda had a routine the babies seemed to accept. They somehow knew, for example, if they were crying at feed time, and they were not picked up immediately, that it was the other twin's turn to be picked up first. Guy or Daisy would lapse into a grizzle just loud enough to keep Magda reminded of their presence. If Vanessa had pangs of jealousy as she watched the calming influence of Magda on the twins, she traded it in for the satisfaction of her complete and ideal life.

One morning, Magda noticed her name on an envelope on the door mat. It shook her to see the hand-written address and the stamp from Poland. It was from the Father Superior. 'Dear Miss Navryk,' he wrote formally, 'I felt it my duty to let you know that your mother has been moved to a sanatorium in Warsaw. Apparently, she has been wandering in the village and upsetting people by asking where Mikal is'.

Magda's guilt at leaving her mother began to eat away inside. Whilst she could think of her mother having some contentment amongst her own people in the village, Magda could cope with that other guilt - the one she had carried around since she was thirteen when Mikal died. Had it not been her fault that he was left in his cot longer than he should have? Hadn't her mother left her in charge whilst she visited her sick sister? And hadn't she been so determined to finish her jigsaw that she left baby Mikal crying for half an hour instead of picking him up to play with him? If she had only picked him up, he wouldn't have had the time to chew on the paint that killed him.

Magda could hardly get through the day, for her churning stomach lurched every time she thought of the letter and the unhappy state of her mother. Every time she picked up Guy or Daisy, she thought of Mikal. She couldn't even powder them that night. The smell was all too poignant.

The next day Vanessa took a rare morning off from the office. Vanessa and Magda were to take the babies for their first vaccinations at the primary care clinic. Eager to experience the maternal regime as part of her whole life experience, Vanessa suggested they walk together with the buggy through the park and on to the clinic. Vanessa heard the birdsong in the park, saw her two beautiful, contented babies and was in expansive mood. 'Don't you ever want to have children or your own Magda?', she smiled with smug satisfaction.

'Yes, of course - it would make my mother very happy', Magda blurted out defensively, not really intending to mention her family troubles as Vanessa liked only clear horizons.

At the clinic there was a hitch. They had to wait for Guy's reaction to one of the vaccines. It would be half an hour. Vanessa's half day was running out. She would go home with Daisy and feed her whilst waiting for Magda and Guy.

So it was that Magda found herself walking back through the park, cuddling Guy against her. She sat down on a bench to get her breath back and lost herself in the baby's gaze. At that moment he chose to give his very first real smile. His right cheek dimpled, his eyes crinkled with glee and he almost appeared to giggle. He was so happy with Magda. Magda was all he needed really. And she needed him to love as he loved her. She needed him to mend the scars her little brother's death had left on her heart. She needed him too, to rescue her mother. Yes, surely her mother could and would recover herself and her happiness when she had something to love again?

As Magda walked on, the baby smiling contentedly up at her, she turned out of the park and towards the tube. Was it really possible? Why not, with God's help? And God only knew her longing and her distress. God would help Magda find a way.

Vanessa waited for one and a half hours before calling the clinic. After that she was at a loss and panicking. For the first time ever, she rang Tim. 'Tim darling. I need you. Please come home. Magda and baby Guy are missing. I don't know what to do.'

On the way home, Tim called the police who were there when he arrived. A very understanding policewoman tried to calm, a by now, hysterical Vanessa and ascertain the facts. 'After all we've done for that young woman! We've given her a home and a lovely job and a salary she would never have had in Poland. It's just greed, that's what it is. She wants my baby, she wants my life!'

The police asked pertinent questions about Magda and her background. Vanessa got out the impeccable reference from the seminary in Poland, but could add little else. 'Do you think she might want to take the baby back to Poland?'
'Oh my God!', sobbed Vanessa, 'She said something about her mother wanting a baby!'.

The police lost no time in contacting the airports and ferry ports. Magda boarded the ferry with the baby at Harwich after withdrawing her savings before leaving London. She breathed a sigh of relief, collapsing into a lounge seat. The captain announced a short delay due to a technical fault. Baby Guy dropped to sleep and Magda was about to do the same.

Then there was a tap on her shoulder.

Vanessa gave evidence in court that they were exemplary employers and that in her opinion, the motivation for kidnapping Guy was greed, pure and simple. The trouble with Magda was she wasn't content with what she had.

The counsel for the defence began to unfold the tale of Magda's youth and family in Poland. When he finished there was a few seconds' silence before the usual coughs and shoe scuffs could be heard again.

Magda was sent to prison for three years for her crime.

Vanessa rose to the top of her profession, smashing the glass ceiling on the way since no woman had ever held a position on the board before.

PRESENT AT THE WEDDING

I heard someone come up the garden path but by the time I had pulled on my dressing gown and padded down to my cottage door, there was no-one there - just some post on the mat. There was the usual Linen Traders' brochure, special offers at the garden centre and the council-tax bill I was dreading as I never quite know where to find the annual (this year, 15%) increase from. I have to budget so carefully these days since retiring that I often wonder why it is that I've never seemed to have those two commodities together - time and money. Either you work your socks off earning your salary or you have all the leisure in the world but not enough money to do anything exciting.

Never mind, it was Oxfam shop day, so I had to get a move on. Well, that's just another example - what do you do in your retirement? You do voluntary work - because it doesn't cost you money and you use up some of your endless time. What is more, there are some perks - you get first dibs of the newly-arrived items before they are steamed and priced for the public. A cog in the wheel of clothes recycling I am.

Well! The post that day brought a surprise all right - an embossed, lined envelope, hand-written in a confident, loose sort of italic style that looked familiar. My toast went cold whilst I worked out who it reminded me of. Sylvie, that's who it reminded me of - a strawberry-blond toss of an immaculate haircut and a plummy accent shot through with French rolling 'r's. 'Well, don't be ridiculous my dear. Of course you must wear nail polish, but only the right sort of Hermès red, or transparent. Nothing else.' I dropped onto the kitchen chair, memories crowding in, completely blotting out the mundanity of Oxfam duty.

Oh, those magical years in Normandy with George. I had invited some new neighbours to drinks at noon one Sunday and nearly cancelled because I had put my back out. George reminded me that it was only a matter of an hour for drinks, so I pulled on some jogging pants despite the pain, and set out some nibbles. As a strawberry blond vision sailed past the front window in a red Chanel jacket, I knew I had lost the sartorial high ground right away.

Sylvie and Roger, (in that order and never Roger and Sylvie, as anybody could see Roger was merely Sylvie's consort) stayed that day until 11pm through bread, pâté and cheese hastily gathered for an impromptu lunch, and tinned confits de canard and roast potatoes for dinner - appreciatively and liberally washed down by a bottle or two of our very best wine.

So despite our differing backgrounds, we all became great friends and Sylvie turned out to be one of those amazing personalities you never forget and who touch your life indelibly. She was full of a zest for life in her mid-fifties that would shame a twenty-something. She would stay late into the night amusing guests with her anecdotes, doing really bad impressions of people she knew, to comic and sometimes scathing effect. She was critical about everything that really didn't matter, yet she maintained that they were of the greatest importance. People who said 'ever so', baguettes baked in a mould, ungrammatical French spoken by the French, anything not BCBG (*bon chic, bon genre* - the French equivalent of U).

I learned so much from Sylvie about life in French bourgeois circles and, although our friendship might have been very superficial, it was not at all. We shared our anxieties and our little successes. Two years later, both of us were widows and back in England. Our friendship continued even though I was back in Lancashire, and Sylvie followed her daughter to London. True to her style, Sylvie started a whole new career in public relations at the age of sixty-one.

I would often drive down and stay at Sylvie's chic little flat in Maida Vale, revelling in the treats she always offered - a meal at L'Escargot, trying wigs on in Selfridges' store, visiting restored houses in the old Huguenot area.

This came to an abrupt end when Sylvie fell ill. I spent days keeping her company and became closer to Thérèse, Sylvie's daughter. Too soon, after only three months, Sylvie died of a very vicious cancer. At last I opened the envelope and read the card:

> *Joshua and Thérèse cordially invite you to their wedding at 3pm on 14th May 2005 at Chelsea Register Office and afterwards at Giorgio's, Mayfair.*
> *RSVP*

My wedding in Mayfair. My wedding! Only six weeks to wait. We'll have all our gang from work and Miles and everybody from uni. It'll be so amazing. It would be great to have it in a church near the restaurant and then all walk through the streets, but I can't be a hypocrite. So, a register office then. Josh won't mind, he's a sweetie. Aw, fancy finding a bloke who's sensitive and talks to me just as much as I want him to, but is still really manly and fanciable. Mind you, it's taken for ever. God, I can't bear to think of the men in my past - losers, the lot of them.

Josh's folks'll have to come, naturally. So how many of them is that? When you count all his parents' cousins (and they're all as thick as thieves) there must be about thirty. He'll have to cut that down to twenty. I'm determined on Mayfair, anyway it's booked, for ninety people. Ninety is just about right - enough to make it a real occasion but not so many that they can't relax and have a good time. Not to be mercenary or anything but hopefully the presents will be really nice ones. I've included some cheapies on the list so that should be okay. I am so lucky. Lucky, lucky, lucky.

Mustn't eat any more brownies - won't be able to get my bum into my amazingly gorgeous dress. No veil, just simple flowers and a really classic satin fitted thirties dress, or should I say gown? Hope it's warmish 'cos I do not intend putting anything on top of my plunging décolleté.

So, back to the job in hand - invitations all piled up and ready to roll. So okay. Joint friends *most* important. Actually I really think they are, when you're not a kid any more, I mean, my uni friends date back, like, fifteen years, and that's almost a generation isn't it? Right, okay then… say twenty for Josh's lot, then mine. OMG! Tante Reine, Oncle Nicholas and their children from France! If they don't mix in with the English, it'll be a disaster! Well anyway, they're really classy, they should certainly raise the tone, as they say. So that's twelve from my side. Is that all? Well, I'm having my wedding in Mayfair even if Mummy can't be here - or Daddy. In fact I mustn't lose sight of the fact that it's because of Mummy's money that I can have a really smart wedding. She would have loved that, they both would, but she the most - my French *maman*. God, do I miss her! I know she'd adore my dress and the restaurant. She wouldn't mind about the register office either since they all have civil weddings in France. Actually she'd be fussing more over her own outfit than mine! She was always so chic. She liked everything just so. And it will be, Mummy, it will be.

What about Elizabeth - mother's friend who came from Lancashire? They were strangely close those two. Elizabeth the teacher and my tall, elegant mother from Paris. I suppose it was the French language that drew them together. I wonder if Elizabeth'd come to my wedding? She was always good at getting my sense of humour. Where does she live these days? Oh, here she is in the book. I hope she's still at this address. I rather like the idea of having her there to sort of stand in for Mummy. I'll get these cards and wedding lists posted this weekend after Josh has agreed to the list. Then that's it really, just the place cards to do (natural linen-backed vellum - very tasteful) and my make-over at Céline's.

What a wonderful surprise! Thérèse was inviting me to her wedding! She wanted to keep in touch! My head rang with so much excitement that I threw on the first top and trousers I set eyes on and scraped my Corsa backing out of my too narrow garage. All the way to the Oxfam shop I mulled over this new adventure. A wedding in Mayfair! Well, well. I had to get my skates on as the wedding was in less than a month.

Well, that day luck was on my side, as the very first dustbin bag of arrivals produced a coffee-coloured dress that fitted snugly over my waist and hips and then fluted out prettily under the knees. I had already seen a cream jacket on the rails with a soft peplum that would go with the dress a treat. The other ladies agreed it was not at all last year's fashion and with a good dry-clean, it would be just the thing. 'Where are you going to stay in London, Elizabeth?', asked one of them. I hadn't thought. I would have to look at the money left that month to be able to make decisions.

'What about the congestion charge they have to pay down there?', said another, 'and parking is almost impossible, they say'.

'What are you going to get her for a present?', was the last question ringing in my ears as I drove home from the dry cleaners having paid £20 for that alone.

Ah, the wedding present. Actually, another sheet had come with the invitation, headed 'Wedding List' which I had tucked behind the clock on the mantel. There were some seventy items on it, in fairly precise detail - all of them available at Harrods. My heart dropped into my stomach. This was why I'd put it out of sight. What had begun as a wonderful adventure was becoming an impossible mountain to climb.

Never mind, I'd find a way. If Thérèse had not really wanted me to be there, she wouldn't have sent the invitation. Young people are refreshingly straightforward like that. What is more, I had an inkling that if we re-forged the link between us, maybe some sort of relationship might emerge. I remembered how Thérèse used to catch my eye at something someone said, that nobody else in the group found amusing. Thérèse had lost both her parents and, you never know, she might like an older woman to talk to now and then. She might even like to come up to Lancashire to escape the hustle and bustle of London for a day or two.

But the more I thought of the wedding list, the more tortured I felt. You were supposed to check off what you were going to buy. Wouldn't that mean you and your present would be put in price rank order? Would the presents be exhibited so that the guests could feel pride or shame on a sliding scale? I could picture the scene - a huge table in a reception hall with raised sections for the biggest, most expensive presents and my humble salt and pepper pots on a corner - except there was nothing as cheap as salt and pepper pots on the list.

As I did the washing-up, I heard Jenni Murray on Women's Hour with two other women, discussing the latest vogue for weddings. 'It's understandable, I suppose. Singletons are now typically in their thirties when they first marry. They have flats or even houses of their own and so they already have two of most things you need to set up a house. What's the use of a third toaster after all? Well, it seems the wedding guest doesn't need to make any difficult decisions about the wedding present now. They are being asked, quite bluntly, to give money - cash. Are we all going to go along with this new wedding etiquette, Lisa?' Just as Jenny said that, I caught myself wiping my rolling pin. It was one of my wedding presents. I pictured Mrs Dale arriving at our back door, forty years before, with that very rolling pin, wrapped in floral paper and white ribbon.

'Always use this for spreading good taste around, Liz, and not for coming to blows with your young man.' I turned the radio off. I would go, I would for Thérèse's sake, and to hell with the cost. I caught the bus the day after into Manchester and went straight to the most expensive store.

I bought some wonderful porcelain crockery - only the dinner plates and side plates, but they were exquisite with the pattern Thérèse had listed, in white, turquoise and dark green and for the first time since I was widowed, I went into the red with my credit card to the tune of £300. I asked the girl to gift-wrap the plates, and was annoyed but amused to be asked to pay £3 extra and come back in an hour. I remembered the wonderful service in France where they would offer to gift wrap a single chocolate, just to please you.

The travel agents were helpful with hotel suggestions, but nothing was available in central London under £200 per night as I really couldn't be far from the Mayfair venue if I had to get back to the hotel on my own. And if I drove down to London I would be too tired to enjoy the wedding unless I went the day before. And there was the car parking to think about. If only George were there, to make light of these silly little obstacles and make life fun again!

In the end, I decided to leave the car at home, ask my next-door neighbour to run me to town and then to take the coach to London. This would save two nights in a hotel as I could come home straight after the reception, with only a taxi to pay.

I can't tell you how relieved I was to have found a feasible solution. I was going! I would have to wear my lovely outfit on the coach, but no matter. Thank goodness it wasn't linen!

So, ten days before the wedding, my lovely cream outfit newly-cleaned and hanging in a plastic cover on the bedroom door, I remembered the wedding present was still in the boot of the car. I decided to bring it indoors ready for leaving, as the car would be locked in the garage.

I shouldn't have tried to close the boot of the car, still struggling with the box, but foolishly I did. The box slipped from my hands and crashed onto the path, smashing everything inside, together with any possibility of going to any wedding anywhere.

I could not face the shame of arriving without the present. I couldn't find the money or the strength to replace it. So I did nothing but cry. It took me two whole days to get out my best writing-paper.

Only a week to go! My nails just have to stay as perfect as they are. Can't wait to see all my family and friends. Oops, sorry, I mean *our* family and friends. Hope I recognise them all. Some I haven't seen for ages. I do hope Mummy's friend Elizabeth enjoys it. I know she will, but I'll have to remember to introduce her to people. She speaks good French so I'll get Jeremy to introduce her to Reine and Nicholas, she'll keep them amused, I know. She's good with kids too, as I remember. I'll just get the post, then I'm off to work.

What's this?

> *Dear Thérèse,*
>
> *I did say I would be coming to your wedding and it would have given me great pleasure to do so. Unfortunately, I haven't been too well lately and I don't think the travelling will do me any good.*
>
> *I'm sorry to have to tell you at the last minute but I do hope your day is very special and that you and Joshua will be very happy together.*
>
> *Yours very sincerely,*
>
> *Elizabeth*

Oh no! She's not coming! Must ring Geraldine to tell her to take the place card away. Damn it! I could have asked Em and Jude, but there's only one place. They're such a hoot and I had to leave them out just to fit her in. Josh! Josh! Guess what? This friend of mother's - she's not coming after all. I mean, if she's been ill, why didn't she say so before. We could have had Em and Jude instead - *so* much more fun. What a waste of an invitation. Really. It's my own fault for being such a soft touch, I know. Well, I'll tell you what, she doesn't deserve to be coming, the silly old trout. No, I don't really mean that, but I'm, like, really disappointed in her, you know? Not even to bother coming to my wedding! Old people are *so* selfish, aren't they?

SAY IT WITH FLOWERS

Kat loitered in the cathedral, stroking the stone-cold feet of a medieval knight. 'And did those feet, in ancient times…', came to her lips, suggesting that the WI may be all the social life she would have from now on. She shook off the thought, calling it mere self-pity. After all, she had coped with Neil's sudden death very well so far. She had had to arrange the funeral to satisfy the whole family and it had turned out to be a succession of surprisingly pleasant family gatherings. With amazing energy she had sorted out Neil's clothes and personal bric-a-brac, and been satisfyingly diplomatic about sharing them out. But then, Kat knew in her heart that after such periods of heightened activity, there usually came a lull, a lull like this, where she could no longer avoid the pits of depression like the one she could feel coming on.

Her mobile jigged its silly jingle. She fished it out of the bottom of her bag whilst avoiding looking at the verger walking about with his long candle-snuffer. 'Hello,' said a mellow, comforting baritone, 'am I speaking to Catherine?'. Kat flinched as she acknowledged her metamorphosis over thirty years from Catherine through Kate to Kat.

'Just a second', was her non-committal reply as she flew out of the Lady Chapel into the dappled sunlight of the graveyard. 'Yes. That's right,' she breathed, 'who's this?'.

'Roger.'

'Oh! Really? R-Roger? H-how are you?' She breathed slowly, pulling together the memories about the only Roger she had ever come across. It could only be him.

'I'm okay. I heard about your loss from one of your relatives and thought I'd ring.'

And whilst he offered his condolences, Kat's mind reeled through all the intervening years when, on 25th March every year, on her birthday, a bouquet of white roses and a card were delivered to her door. There was never anything really objectionable on the card to upset her husband - 'with the best of wishes' or 'with such happy memories' it would say, and Neil knew he couldn't object. Indeed, Kat's sister once remarked to Neil that he was a very lucky man, having landed a wife who was obviously desirable to others. For some years, the arrival of the flowers came as a romantic surprise then it became a family joke. Neil would comment on the lines of, 'Flowers from your secret admirer again. Fancy that!'.

'So, will you?', Roger's soft voice interrupted.

'Sorry, will I what?' Kat juggled with her mobile and put it to her other ear.

'Meet me for lunch. We go back a long way, Catherine, and I've waited a long time to see you again. I never forgot you did I? You surely owe me this?'

Kat found herself without an argument to the contrary. After all, what harm could there be? Here was a man who, although he had only met her twice when they were gauche teenagers at the local dance hall, had sent her a card and flowers every year on her birthday since. Even though she had accepted his request to dance to 'do the locomotion with me', she had rejected his offer to walk her home that night after the DJ announced her birthday. So, why the cards and the flowers and why would he want to meet her now? Was it that he knew she was officially single now and he truly wanted to pursue a relationship with her? And then there was her own curiosity. Who could not want to see the man whom she last saw as a twenty-year-old, who had asked her out but never even kissed her? Who would say no in her position right now?

There was only one set of traffic lights between the cathedral close and home, yet Kat failed to stop at the red light. Luckily no other cars were about. 'Get a grip, Kat!', she muttered. Was she just excited at the prospect of seeing an old acquaintance again or did she feel guilty because this Roger was more of an old flame than anything else - he certainly wasn't a friend. She backed the car into the garage.

Her mobile rang again. 'Hello mum. How's things? Would you like to come over for lunch on Sunday? We thought we'd have a barbecue whilst the forecast's good.'
'Um. Bee, it's a lovely thought, but I can't. I've so much to do before Aunty Dorothy comes next week.'
'Oh… shall I come over on Saturday to help?'
'No. No. Don't you worry. I like having lots to do. You know how it is…'
'Now why should I feel guilty for having a little pleasure in my life?', Kat's thoughts began. 'I nursed Neil for months this last year without counting all the years I was… what?' What had she been? A golf widow that's what she had been. It was so accepted, so normal, that Neil was a keen golfer and shouldn't be expected to sacrifice his leisure pursuit, especially since he had worked over forty years at a desk to keep them all in moderate comfort.

The train of thought continued as Kat pummelled the feather pillows in the spare room. 'Come to think of it, you could say those flowers got me through thirty years of what could have been a very boring married life. It's just as well they brought a buzz into my existence. I suppose nowadays women would be reading Fifty Shades of Grey!' She patted her hair and decided to book an appointment at the expensive salon in town.

The following Saturday morning Kat looked at herself in the mirror. 'Well, I might not be whistled at by the workmen in the street any more but I certainly feel better about myself. What did that questionnaire in this week's magazine ask? "Are you a glass half full, or a glass half empty sort of person?". Well if it were not for those flowers telling me once a year and every year that I was admired and thought of as special, who knows? My glass might have been drained to the dregs by now. So I'm going to thank you Roger for letting me smell the roses!'

The Saracen's Head in a country village exuded quiet confidence and delicious smells. Kat stepped through two sets of glass doors and then stood, straightened her back, and looked around to get her bearings. There were couples at smaller tables and two or three families at larger ones dotted around the room but no sight of a single man looking for her arrival. Then she glimpsed a woman in the far corner between two windows, looking over and raising a hand commandingly.

Kat approached apologetically and spoke first. 'Hello. I'm afraid there's a mistake. I'm waiting for…'
'There's no mistake,' the woman's strident voice asserted, 'and he's over there near the door. You just walked past him'. Kat turned to see a tall man with sloping shoulders and a few remaining wisps of grey around his neckline, like a tonsure fallen from grace. Could this chap really be Roger of the flowers? That amazing-looking boy with a

blond quiff like David Bowie, who had looked so cool Kat had shrunk back and refused his approaches, convinced he could have had any girl in the dance hall?

But who was this smart woman at the table, beginning to command the situation? After handshakes, one nervous and one firm, Kat felt she had to win the next round, so she kick-started the curious conversation by showing an interest, as women do, in the man's business. The subject threatened to monopolise as Roger warmed to his theme, seemingly oblivious to the antagonism flowing between the two women. The smart one swung round to her husband. Her dyed-black bob bounced on her square jaw. Her diamond earrings glittered no more than her eyes. 'Yes Rog. I'm sure Catherine would love to know more but could we get something to eat, today? By the way, Catherine, I'm Alice. How do you do?', she announced, holding forth a bejewelled, purple-nailed hand. Kat obediently took the hand, mentally kicking herself for giving in to this woman who had obviously found out where her husband was going and was determined to humiliate him and Kat alike.

They variously ordered a small starter, fish and chips and oysters and when the food arrived they had little to say - were they all, like Kat, churning the situation over and over? The clatter of cutlery hardly cutting the tension, Roger looked up from his plate several times and seemed puzzled by Kat's appearance. 'You didn't used to wear glasses did you?', he said, disappointment leaking from his watery eyes.
'What does he expect?', thought Kat. 'No - my hair isn't flowing long and blond and I'm not a size ten any more, but have you looked in the mirror lately?' She struggled to keep her smile in place. Then Kat tried to regain her slipping composure, save her pride and turn the conversation away from herself.
'And what do you two enjoy doing in your spare time? Do you travel much?'

'I'd love to, but it takes two to tango, doesn't it, dear?', replied Alice with a visible curl to the matching purple lipstick.

'You know you can, anytime you want to. I wouldn't stop you.' Roger's voice trailed off.

'The truth is, Catherine, that Roger's happiest with his little machines. He's at work every day he can be. Anyway, what about you? How long did you and Roger go out together?' This took Kat by surprise and she looked at Roger for a clue. His face was expressionless, his eyes directed at the floor.

'I might as well not be here', thought Kat. 'Come to think of it, why am I here? Why did I spend so much time in the attic drooling over the cards I'd collected over the years from him? Why did I not spend more time with Neil? Didn't he take up golf the year after that awful row we'd had about our respective girlfriends and boyfriends?'

'Go on. You can tell me. We're all grown up now', Alice persisted.

'But I… we, hardly…' Kat shuffled and looked at her wedding ring for inspiration. Roger looked up at last, a blush slowly rising from his collar.

'It was only a date, Alice - just once if you must know', the blush rushed over his eyes, making two red pools. 'I thought you'd never fancy me if you knew that I'd never had a real girlfriend. That's why I thought of sending some flowers on Catherine's birthday.'

'So you were trying to make me jealous all these years?'

'It started that way, but since it didn't succeed, I carried on in the hope of provoking some emotion - any kind of reaction really.' Not a muscle moved on Alice's face.

'I didn't choose you to satisfy my emotions, Roger.' Her voice dropped to a stage whisper.

Both of them were staring at their plates. Kat too, as she thought of all those years when she had gradually dried up her affection and love for Neil, only to have spent the last twenty of them in a loveless marriage. And whose fault was it? Was it really Neil's, as she always claimed? Kat stood up slowly. 'This is where I take my leave', she said quietly. She picked up her handbag and walked over to reception, saying over her shoulder, 'I'll settle the bill'.

SECRET PASSIONS

Well, well. They've pulled down the old convent grammar to build an 'executive' housing estate. The end of an era. Unlike those stones, the memories of at least ten thousand adolescent girls are not so easily demolished. I remember so clearly Sister Theresa's soft voice that always pierced my heart. 'Patricia - paragraph four, page seventy-two please.' I grimaced as I tried to keep my thoughts on the text.

'Sorry sister... um... Saint Edmund Campion was hung, drawn and quartered for professing the true faith. The victim was hung from a scaffold; his body was taken down within seconds so that he would still be alive and the executioner carved open his belly so deeply the intestines spurted out, blood splashing those close by. The executioner then carved the victim literally into quarters, a limb attached to each quarter. The head was usually driven onto a pike and these macabre exhibits were placed at the gates to the city "pour encourager les autres".' Feeling nauseous, I stumbled over the French phrase. Sister repeated it immaculately, as she did everything.

I would have felt even sicker had my attention not been distracted earlier by the sight of a wisp of light brown hair which had escaped from sister's wimple. Of course she would be fair-haired. Sister's eyebrows were perfect light-brown arches over lids so delicate you could see the veins pulse slightly when sister's eyes lowered to her text. Her veil framed her face as in a medieval painting. Her features were controlled, calm - all unnecessary movements eliminated. 'Of course,' added sister to the morose and silent class, 'the holy martyrs were chosen to suffer for Our Lord. Their reward was waiting for them in heaven. Remember too, girls, that their suffering was nothing to that suffered by Jesus on Calvary'. At the name of Jesus, she inclined her head slowly and slightly. Only the initiated would notice.

I adored Sister Theresa's control, calm and delicacy. My own hair grew in two heavy plaits that thumped on my back as I took a pass and ran at netball. My face was usually flushed with excitement or embarrassment. My movements were dictated by emotions, feet tapping in impatience, bumping into things in my eagerness to please, nail-biting in anxiety. If only I could be like Sister Theresa. I used to think if I watched her closely, I would learn the secrets of that awesome collectedness which surely meant you had found the path to heaven and true happiness.

When the bell went, nobody moved. We all knew to wait until Sister stood and with a tiny upward gesture of one hand, signalled the girls to stand and chant, 'Thank You Sister Mary Theresa', then watch as she glided out of the classroom. Only then could we file out.
'I saw you Pat,' sniggered Margaret, 'you can't take your eyes off sister can you? You've definitely got a pash on her!'.
'Oh, grow up!', I muttered, without conviction.

We fifth-formers, old enough to curb our hunger pangs, were on second sitting for lunch and that day I was extra hungry having had a game of tennis. This had been strangely unenjoyable because the thought had struck me that hitting a ball might be an aggressive and indelicate act for a would-be nun. Yet what saintly way could there be to return the ball over the net?

In the canteen queue, I calmed my thoughts and deliberately spoke more quietly. I took my napkin and spread it carefully on my lap. The duty teacher clapped her hands and three hundred girls fell silent for grace. As I mouthed the prayer, one word lingered in my mind - denial. This was what I must do. Deny myself, conquer my weak body and refuse to allow it to dictate my behaviour. In that way, I would become sweeter, lovelier, and holier - like Sister Mary Theresa.

My first opportunity lay before me. As the prefect at the head of the table passed down the serving dishes of cabbage, potatoes and fatty pork in Bisto, I took just one spoonful of each. 'Crikey. You're not dieting are you Pat?' Margaret never missed a trick.
'Course not. I... I'm not interested in how I look.' It was my first statement on the narrow path to holiness. I glowed inside.
'You will be when you see how fab Lulu looks at the Mecca next week!', grinned Margaret.
'I'm not going.' It no longer fitted the image I wanted of myself and anyway, my mother wouldn't let me.

After lessons, humping my school-case and hockey stick up the corridor towards the exit, I turned the last corner and almost bumped into Sister Mary Theresa. 'Oh, erm, I'm *so, so*, very sorry Sister.' The words came out in a breathless staccato. Sister looked somewhere in the region of my shoulder, nodded gravely and glided on, holding her rosary in her left hand to prevent it clinking unnecessarily.

The mortification of my pathetic apology left me in a low mood on the way home. Derek, the newspaper boy, cycled past and turned to look at me as I got off the bus. 'Hiya, Pat,' he grinned, 'going to the Mecca next Saturday?'.

For at least a year, I had day-dreamed of Derek and had joined the village band, even when the only instrument they could let me have was the French horn, just to be able to watch Derek triple-tonguing the top line in Trumpet Voluntary on the cornet. During the religious retreat at school, we had all been told that one could commit sin in thought as well as deed. I had confessed to Father Peter, kneeling by the armchair in Mother Superior's study, where Father had ensconced himself for the three days' retreat. 'You must control your thoughts my child. Nothing is hidden from The Almighty. Keep yourself from temptation.'

'Is that you, Patricia?', shouted Mother from the sitting-room as I came in the front door. Being an only child, her question irritated me. Who else would it be? 'Get your riding stuff together, your lesson's at five', came the instruction.

'I thought it was cancelled.'

'Well, I've rung the stables and Sebastian says he can fit us in at five. Do get a move on!'

At the stables, I went through the motions but somehow the old thrill of animal nearness no longer satisfied me. The smell of the sweating horse, the rubbing of my thighs on the saddle, felt too earthy. I now craved something on a higher plane to satisfy my heart and mind. It was like being ten again and out playing with my friends who were making mud pies. Suddenly I had realised how childish it was. It had been time to move on. At about that time, I had started watching Princess Anne when she appeared on television and five years' horse-riding had followed. Now, even that seemed childish and faintly repugnant.

I was positively relieved when I had rubbed the horse down and could go. I collected my hat, and came out into the yard to see my mother talking to the manager, as she seemed to do most riding days. Mother was smiling, curling her foot round her other ankle. Sebastian was talking quietly at her side, looking at the ground and tapping his riding whip against his boot. I realised it was the only time I ever saw Mother smile. How would I tell her I wanted to give up riding?

As soon as I could, I went up to my bedroom and took down all my posters of horses and put them in a cardboard box under my bed. Thomas A Kempis' 'The Imitation of Christ' replaced my favourite book 'Black Beauty'. My bookmark was now a picture of Our Lady and I used this to rest my finger on when reading. I had once asked one of the nuns why they did this and was told it was to avoid wearing out the page unnecessarily. Under the crucifix on the wall, I put a little statue of Saint Theresa of Lisieux that Dad had bought me at the church bring-and-buy sale. Dad's favourite record was Malcolm Vaughan singing 'St. Therese of the Roses'. He played it often in the shed on a wind-up gramophone when he was mending his fishing tackle.

The front door opened and shut underneath my little bedroom which meant Dad was home. There was no call from the kitchen, just a cacophony of pans and cutlery as Mother reluctantly threw herself into action. 'Have you had a nice day, dear?', asked Dad at dinner-time to anyone who would reply.
'Yes Dad. I played some tennis at lunch time and the girls were singing on the bus on the way home. It was a gas', I said, light-heartedly as usual because I knew he wanted me to be happy. That was why he worked in the factory office every day from eight thirty to five, he said - to keep his girls happy.
'There's no pudding if you don't finish your greens', announced Mother.

Dad left the table to go to his shed. He had a collection of over one hundred and fifty different fishing flies, each one of which he could explain the colour and purpose of, if anyone would let him. Most weekends, he took himself off fishing. I had been with him once or twice and found the activity incomprehensible even though he explained it was his way of getting away from the world and its stresses. 'Just relax and listen to the birds. Those tiny splashes of water tell you where the fish are. Let nature take over. When you cast your line, you cast off your worries, see?' How careful he was to choose just the right fly, how patient he was just waiting for the twitch on the line and how skilful he was reeling in a fish when he got a bite. He would stroke the fish when he had landed it, weigh it in his hands, look it in the eye, then throw it back again. It was a passion I would never understand.

That night in my room, I concentrated on my rosary, 'The Sorrowful Mysteries' for Good Friday. But after 'The Agony in the Garden', and 'The Scourging at the Pillar', I felt drained and just had to switch on my new transistor radio. I fell asleep to The Everley Brothers singing, 'Dream... dream, dream, dream, dream, dream...'. Tomorrow I would do better.

The next morning, Mother brushed my hair in her usual vigorous fashion. 'Stimulates the follicles', she muttered. She parted my thick hair from forehead to nape in one long drag of the steel comb and each side of my head was fingered into three strands which Mother expertly whipped over and over then imprisoned in a strong rubber band. As she worked on the second plait, Dad shouted from the hallway,
'I'm off dear'. Mother yanked the strands tighter. I wouldn't have to put up with this in a convent, I thought.

At lunch time I was determined to test my new-found vocation and cried off from tennis, much to Margaret's dismay. 'What's wrong with you, Pat? Are you mooning over some boy?'
'You're disgusting, Maggie', I flung out, knowing she hated being

called Maggie. I knew at once that that was one more for my next confession.

Although the girls were allowed to avail themselves of the chapel for private prayer at lunchtimes, hardly anyone ever did. It was Maundy Thursday, the last day of term and so, appropriately, I decided to do the Stations of the Cross. It was meant to be particularly uplifting because you got to move from one picture to another in your progress around the chapel, just like Christ on Calvary. I had never had the opportunity to do this on my own before. 'Bless you child,' smiled Mother Superior, who was standing inside the door, 'and you haven't even had lunch'. I made my way to the first plaster-cast picture on the wall of the chapel.

Soon I was contemplating the agonies that Christ suffered and was humbled. Then I came to the depiction of the soldiers forcing the crown of thorns on Jesus' head and blood pouring down his face and I felt anything but uplifted. I was reminded of the fish with the hook through its lip. The scourging of Christ deepened the feeling of repulsion. Why did God allow this to happen? I turned away from the blood. The picture where the soldiers take a hammer and bang nails though Jesus' hands and feet to fix him to the cross was the last straw. I was nauseated. I felt like a voyeur. If there had been this dreadful suffering, why make a Technicolor performance of it?

I didn't complete the fourteen stations. I ran out and once again, almost bumped into Sister Mary Theresa. I didn't speak this time as I was holding back the vomit until I reached the flower bed outside the chapel. For the first time, I felt revulsion at the idolatry of violence. How could I ever be a nun if it meant contemplating the macabre and the cruel for the rest of my life? 'I forgive you my child, for your earlier impertinence,' mocked Margaret, swinging her tennis racket as she crossed the lawn, 'I'll just call you petty Patty from now on'.

I wiped my mouth with my sleeve and shouted back, 'Call me what you like Marg, but I'm coming with you next week to the Mecca. I don't care what my mum says!'.

'Great!', shrieked Margaret, 'My mum will let me go if you can go. She knows you never do anything wrong!'.

On the way out of school I passed the chapel, where the few resident nuns filled two benches with their clear, untrammelled voices. For Sister Theresa, any transition was from the outside world to her interior one. She continually told us that our minds were full of trivia and worldliness. She herself had had her moment of epiphany when she was fifteen in a wayside grotto in County Clare. Since then, Sister Theresa had dedicated her life to the deepening of her inner faith. Now, more and more it seemed, teaching was getting in the way of her real vocation and she longed for those times when she could give herself entirely to Our Blessed Lord.

On the school bus home it was the last day of term and the girls' spirits were rising. 'Got myself a cryin', talkin', sleepin', walkin', livin' doll', chorused Margaret and some fourth formers, swaying from side to side on their seats, hats plonked on the backs of heads. Their song was soon drowned by the prefects upstairs, who lead the idolising younger girls with their end of term favourite.

'Oh you'll never get to heaven, in Miss Bailey's car, 'cos Miss Bailey's car, won't get that far', and on and on for fourteen verses, each one highlighting a teacher's particular idiosyncrasy.

I somehow couldn't resist the gaiety of the singing and the laughter of my friends and soon I was joining in. My upbeat mood carried me home and even before I flung my school hat onto the hall stand and unbuttoned my coat, I shouted to Mother, 'Margaret's going to her grandmother's in town on Saturday and staying the night. She's invited me too. Can I go... please, please?'.

'Well, I don't see why not, Trisha, it will fit in with my plans too. You see, your father will be away fishing for the weekend and I have offered to help at the stables. You know, decorating the big barn for the barn dance the week after. You know Sebastian does simply everything over there and anyway he might give you extra lessons. You know you could do with some.' I didn't demur. I knew the riding lessons were the price I had to pay for my taste of freedom.

Up in my room, I tuned into Radio Luxemburg and defiantly rummaged around under the bed for some Valentine comics to read. For a while, the guilt of my lie and my betrayal of Christ's call tormented me, but not for long. Soon, sweet thoughts of dancing with a boy and the possibility of a kiss swept me into dreamland.

Years later, having married the newspaper boy and had two children, I went to an old girls' reunion - not at the school, which had already been subsumed into a local comprehensive, but at Margaret's house. I had found her thanks to the website Friends Reunited. We soon fell to reminiscing about the strange pull religion had had on our young minds and I discovered I was not the only girl to have imagined she had a vocation for the religious life. The thought sobered us. Then Margaret dropped the bombshell. 'Did you know that some of the nuns used to self-harm?'
'What on earth are you talking about?', I exclaimed.
'Yes. Even your precious Sister Mary Theresa. My gran was a cleaner at the convent and she told my mum she had seen little leather whips, whips with hooks on the end of the thongs. She wondered what they were for until she opened a door to clean a "cell", as they called them, and actually saw a young nun kneeling in front of a little shrine and whipping herself over her bare shoulders.'
'Good God!', 'Holy shit!' and 'Christ almighty!' were some of the comments.
'Well, everybody has to get their kicks somehow, don't they?', smiled Margaret.

TEDDY BOY

She hadn't been waiting long when her attention was attracted by one of the Italian waiters grinding an enormous pepper pot in front of a woman at a neighbouring table. The woman was giggling and kissing a toy dog on her knee. Size doesn't matter! Helen was dying to tell the old joke, but decided that would be sinking to their level. What's with the toy dog, anyway? Grow up lady! Helen's down-to-earth view of life extended to other people's lives too.

So her attention had strayed when a warm masculine voice next to her spoke. 'It's Helen isn't it?' She looked up in surprise as a pair of chestnut brown eyes held her gaze.

'Yes. Helen Holden.' She thrust her hand upwards to shake his and managed to knock the menu stand onto the floor. Good Lord! He must think I'm a clumsy clown already!

She smoothed down her straight skirt over her knees and flicked out the glossy locks of ash-blond hair caught under her coat collar. 'So you must be George', she said, feeling a bit embarrassed.

'Got it in one. How did you guess?', he teased, looking straight into her eyes again for a moment. Then he let her off the hook by picking up the menu stand and placing it back on the table. 'Let's order something to eat. It'll help us relax', he said. And it did.

George seemed to enjoy the Italian ambiance and even ventured the odd 'grazie' and 'per favore', which delighted the waiter, and made Helen glad she hadn't said anything rude about the pepper pot.

By the time they were tussling with platefuls of spaghetti, which she would never order on a first date, Helen actually felt relaxed enough to giggle as she wiped her orange-stained chin. 'You've missed a bit', George laughed. 'Here!' He took his napkin and wiped her chin, smiling as he did so.

They walked back to the nearest tube station hand in hand. 'Careful!', he grinned as she nearly bumped into a lamp-post. When her train came in, he said goodbye and brushed his lips over her cheek. 'Lovely hint of Bolognese...', he whispered in her ear and put her on the train.

I think it's going to be different this time, thought Helen as she looked out of the window and used it as a screen to replay the evening in her imagination. The way George had been concerned about her comfort, had stroked her arm when she coughed as some food went down the wrong way and had insisted on paying the bill but hadn't insisted on taking her back to her flat. All in good time, she thought.

Suddenly, there was a tap on the window. 'Will you see me again?', George gasped, running along the platform as the train pulled out, 'Or is this just a brief encounter?'.
'No - of course not,' Helen replied, 'how about next week, same time...?'.

'But not the same place?', he shouted. He was beginning to lose ground. 'How about an Indian next time?'

'That would be lovely.' She sat back and reflected how differently things were turning out, even though she had promised herself not to be too keen.

It was some weeks later, after the delicate cooking of a gourmet French restaurant that George wondered aloud if Helen would like to come back to his flat which, as luck would have it, was only a stroll away. George hadn't rushed the moment at all. Indeed Helen was beginning to think she might have to do the asking. This man was so different from David. Her ex had been the reliable, upright and hard-working partner her parents had wanted for her. They had lasted eight years together and when Helen summoned up the courage to be true to herself and admit she didn't love him, couldn't love him, she tried to explain it to her mother. 'It's not that there was anything wrong with David, Mum, but I need more... well more loving from a man. No, I don't really mean sex, I mean... well I suppose I mean affection. He could never show his feelings for me. Maybe he will for someone else, but I know if we'd have had children and I'd had to stay for the next twenty years, I simply couldn't do it. I mean, there's something wrong isn't there when a young woman tries time after time to seduce her lover and he doesn't seem able to respond?'

Helen had already had enough evidence from George, of those tender signs of an expressive and loving nature that she longed for. The way he hugged her to him walking in the street or stroked her knee next to his in the cinema, even the dullest of films was worth sitting through for the thrill of that. So Helen said yes and they strolled back to his flat which was only one floor up from the street with a balcony overlooking the river at the back.

The little almond biscuits with the coffee were a nice touch and made up for the slightly messy flat which was furnished but with big squishy sofas, pictures and photos on every wall and books on every surface, and naturally, a huge television screen dominating the living-room. Helen admitted to herself that the superficial messiness of the flat was a sign that George wasn't too perfect. When she asked to use the bathroom, she knew instinctively that he would jump up from the sofa. 'Course! Hang on a minute though, I just need to…' She could just visualise him gathering stuff from the floor and giving the room an extra spray. Helen chuckled when he came out.

'Ah,' thought Helen, 'your flat may not be perfect but I think you might be perfect - for me'. And if she didn't really say it, her eyes said it for her. George took her hand and intertwined his fingers with hers. His eyes slowly closed as his lips moved softly towards hers and the warmth and smell of his clean and manly skin mingled with her faint aroma of Air du Temps.

Helen felt her heart melting inside as she pulled back to look into his eyes. Just then two other eyes, cold and glassy, to the left of George's head stared straight at her face, just like George was doing. 'Oh God no!', thought Helen.
'What is it?', asked George dreamily, turning round to where her gaze was fixed on a scruffy old teddy bear sitting on a bookshelf behind him. 'Ah, don't mind him, he shouldn't be here,' winked George, and grabbing the furry little thing by its ear, he added, 'it's past your bedtime, mate', and flung it through an open door onto a bed. 'Come here', he continued, stroking Helen's hair and leaning in to kiss her again. But the moment had gone.

He's still got a teddy bear! I could put up with a disordered flat with higgledy-piggledy bookshelves but to have a manky kid's toy stuck there? Oh no! Heavens above, I had thrown away my dolls by the time I was ten and had discovered Jane Austen. 'More coffee?', suggested George, picking up the coffee-jug. 'Are you okay, love?'

'Yeah, yeah,' she answered, 'but it's getting late. I've just remembered a report I've got to submit by tomorrow. Sorry, must go. Don't worry, George, I'll get a taxi on the corner'.

In less than a minute, Helen had put on her jacket, gathered her bag and scarf and scuttled down the stairs. When she looked back up the stairs, she saw George looking down, his jaw sagging.

'You look miles away, Helen. You worried about the review?', asked Josie back at the office.

'Er, what? No, no. I've classified all the paperwork I need to take in with me and I'll fight my corner with the board okay. It's just something personal. Nothing important really, it's just that... well, can I ask you, Josie, do you still have any stuff from when you were a kid - like furry toys and that? For example, do you have cuddly toys on your bed or anywhere?'

'No way. I wouldn't have the patience to throw them off every night to make room for Gary and me - and then put them all back the next morning. Same with all those ridiculous pillows and cushions you see in the furniture shops.'

'Me too. I agree, Josie. But how would you feel if someone you're dating - this significant someone, and he turned out to have an old teddy bear in his living room?'

'If I had cuddly toys on the bed, I should think Gary would kick them into touch pronto. Why, has the new man got a teddy bear, then? Ugh, that's like Sebastian Flyte in Brideshead Revisited. 'Nuff said hey?'

Helen dealt with her annual review without a second thought and came out with the promise of a pay rise. If only personal stuff was that easy. She should, if her usual logic was applied, put George on the back burner and get out there and meet other men, but whenever there was a lull in pressing matters at work, or between her favourite TV programmes, her mind raced back to George and the laughs they had had, the teasing and those quiet moments when they didn't even need to speak to feel good together. It was quite clear though, that George wasn't missing her. He had not rung, texted or contacted her in any way. How hurtful was that?

If this were a work situation, Helen would find the right strategy to move forward without losing face, to see if she could bring the other person round to her point of view. And so she did. She would invite George to dinner - not at a restaurant, but to her flat. She would cook dinner for him, the way to a man's heart and all that, at the same time letting him appreciate the pleasure of a well-ordered home where there was nothing to spoil the image she presented as an independent, mature and desirable woman. 'Dinner at yours?', George repeated. 'But I thought you…'

'I was under a lot of pressure at work, George. I'd like to make it up to you though. What do you think? Could you make it on Friday?'

The days flew by. Helen bought new cushions, a mirror and a lamp, to give the latest look to her living-room and brushed up on her favourite lamb biryani recipe. Friday came and all was ready. The phone rang. 'Oh no! He's going to cancel', thought Helen.

'Hello love,' came her mother's voice, 'I've been mulling over our conversation about David the other week. I've been really upset to think you didn't get the loving you needed from him. It was just the same for me - your dad was very uptight and inhibited, but in those days, divorce wasn't an option. In fact I felt there was something wrong with me being so needy. If I hadn't had you to love, I don't know what I'd have done'.

'Oh Mum, that is so sad. I remember I had to do well at school or pass piano exams and then Dad would buy me presents. But I was like you, it wasn't really the presents I needed, I needed his time and affection.' The doorbell rang.

'I love you lots, Mum. I'll always be there for you.'

'Go and answer the door, Helen. Speak to you soon!', her mother laughed.

'Don't cut off your mum for me,' said George, closing the door behind him and throwing a brown paper bag on the sofa, 'you're lucky to have her'.

'It's all right, I'll phone her back later', said Helen. She bent to pick up the paper bag and put it on the table by the door where it should be.

'That's for you Helen. It's not to keep though, just a little something to explain my life to you.' Helen opened the bag, and took out the teddy bear, not quite understanding. His life? She couldn't put it down in case it looked like she was rejecting it, and therefore George. So she was left holding it and seeing what the years had done to it - an ear missing and odd stitches here and there in the grubby fur.

'You see, Helen. I didn't have a mum. Well, not after I was five. She died of cancer. I never saw my dad - he was killed in a farming accident by a tractor before I was born. So, my grandparents took me in and brought me up on their farm. My teddy bear is the only thing that came with me from my mum's house. Apparently, I wouldn't talk about my mum - granny told me I couldn't forgive her for dying on me. So it was my teddy bear that got all my affection for a long time - until granny just wore me down with the love she poured on me. Not money, not things, they were dirt poor, but love. Strong love. Sometimes tough love. Always tender love. Especially when granddad died too and I was all granny had left. We had to leave the farm and move into the town but it was all right, granny was there and so was my teddy bear. They saw me all the way through university. Now she's gone too, he is my only family. But because of him - why, I feel I've got a surplus of love now and I need somebody who needs my kind of love. I thought it was you, Helen. I thought you were beginning to know me and want what I can give you. Maybe I was wrong.' Helen looked down at the bear thoughtfully. Now she started to stroke it.

'Oh yes. I mean, No, you're not wrong. You're so right. George I do need you. I even think my mum was about to tell me that too.' She stroked the teddy bear again. She was sure it winked right back at her. 'Let's have something to eat. It'll get easier then', Helen whispered.

And it did.

THAT WITCH'S SCISSORS

'That must be her, the woman at the bottom of the street! Don't you get it? She's always cutting people's hair and she's never a hairdresser either. I've seen her in the back garden, putting a pudding basin on somebody's head and cutting round it', said Sam, wiping his nose on his sleeve.

'Yeah,' replied Tom, scrunching up his freckled face, 'I know somebody whose hair she cut and she cut a bit of his ear off as well! I wonder what she does with all those bits of ear she cuts off? Ew! Scary!'.

And so it was that they picked on her. She wasn't very pretty, that's true, and the pimple at the end of her nose exaggerated the effect. Sam and Tom, no more than nine years old or so, reckoned it was their duty to keep this witch's evil at bay and fight the good fight. Tom saw her garden broom leaning against the gate and took it to the gang hut where he ceremoniously pulled out half of the bristles before he put it back in her garden. 'That way, she can't fly off in a hurry', Tom told Sam.

Sam tied one end of a string from her front doorknob to the doorknob on the opposite side of the street, and then Sam's sister Jeanie knocked on both doors one after the other. Watching from round the corner the three of them laughed when, as soon as the opposite door was pulled open, the witch's door slammed shut. 'Serve her right!', declared Tom. Tom was certain he was right because of what they learned at the church at the top of the street, for all things supernatural were the work of Satan and if it says so in the Bible it must be true.

One bonfire week, the little gang were going around the neighbourhood singing, 'Remember, remember…', and forgot about Mrs Black the witch until they got to the bottom of the street, and then they remembered and hammered on her door, giggling. They nudged each other saying, 'Mrs Black! Do you get it? It's the colour of sin and the Devil', when she opened the door. The light from the street lamp reflected off the scissors she was holding and Tom gasped at the thought of a small mountain of bits of ears somewhere in that house.
'Look at that false smile', thought Tom as she opened the door. He shook his head at the bonfire toffee that she passed around to the others.

Those glinting scissors featured in Tom's dreams for a night or two and then it struck him that he had to get the satanic power away from her and that to do so, he would have to get her scissors. 'They must be like a sort of magic wand that helps her curses work better', he shuddered. The rest of the gang weren't so keen, probably because they were bought off by the bonfire toffee - a bit like Judas Tom thought, so he decided to see it through himself. She would have to surrender the scissors or he would have to seize them.

He took to keeping watch by her back-garden gate. At first, if she saw him, she smiled that crooked smile and said, 'You're Johnny, aren't you?'. He never replied of course, as that would put him under her spell. Then she took to telling him to clear off, so he hid round the corner and came back later. Once he saw her cutting someone's hair. It was one of the dirty kids who lived in the back-to-backs. Tom and his gang weren't allowed to play with them.

'There,' the witch said to the kid, 'don't you look the business?'. What business? Whose dirty business was that? Surely the Devil's!

In fact, Tom wasn't sleeping well at all. He told his mum what he had heard her say. She turned from the washing-up in the sink and wiping her hands on her pinny, tried to make sense of it. 'Mrs Black must have said "Don't you look the bee's knees?"', his mother replied, 'That means you look smart. Anyway, Mrs Black is certainly not a witch, she's a widow and that's quite a different thing. Now you be nice to her or you'll get the back of my hand!'.

'They never understand - mums', thought Tom, as he rubbed his shoes on the back of his long socks on the way to Sunday school, 'well, mine wouldn't, would she? She sends me off to Sunday school every week, but does she come to church as well? No - she's going for a natter at her sister's while I have to listen to the vicar droning on for ages until we get called in to Sunday school with Miss Simms'.

It was around Easter time and Tom had a hot cross bun in his hand as he craned his neck to spy through the back-garden gate. The kitchen window was wide open and this time the sunlight was shining right on those scissors. They were on the wooden draining-board at the side of the sink. He crept into the garden and crouched under the window. She was singing, 'Immoral, invisible, God only lies…'.

'What?', thought Tom, clapping a hand over his mouth to stop himself screaming, 'God - immoral? What? God lies? How can God lie? How can God be immoral? This woman is definitely a wicked witch, not a widow'. He reached in and grabbed the scissors and ran out of the gate. Straight away the singing stopped. Just like that, in mid-sentence. He had done it. He had destroyed her power! He had conquered the Devil!

But his elation was short-lived. Yes, he had proved he was worthy of the Lord, but what do you do with a pair of witch's scissors when you've got them? He didn't want to keep them, that's for sure. He didn't even want to touch them any longer than he had to, and if he gave them to anybody, they would be jinxed for ever. So he decided simply to throw them away. 'I hope Mum doesn't see me', he thought, as he lifted the dustbin lid in the backyard. 'She never wastes anything. How will I explain this? She once caught me crumpling up the margarine paper without scraping it with a knife and gave me a clip round the ear.' Sure enough, her voice rang out from the kitchen. 'Thomas! What do you think you're doing? Where did you get those?' Well, Tom held out as long as he could - about five minutes, during which time she threatened him with blue murder, but then he blurted it all out, tears streaming down his face.

She went white. Then she sat him down in his dad's armchair and stroked his cheek. She gently explained that Mrs Black's husband had died and that she did nothing but good in the neighbourhood. 'I know she doesn't go to church but you don't have to go to church to be good', she said. She went on, 'Mrs Black used to be a hairdresser before she retired and now she gives free haircuts to all the poor people who live in the back-to-backs'. His mother marched him down to Mrs Black's front door and knocked for Tom to say he was sorry.

'So why is she crying when it's me who's in trouble?', muttered Tom to himself.

One Sunday school class, Miss Simms explained they were going to have a question box. They were to write any question they had about

God or the Church on a piece of paper and she told them that spelling didn't matter (which amazed Tom because it was the only time any teacher had ever said that). In that way, she explained, they need not feel embarrassed by their questions. They all thought a lot and bit their pencils, and afterwards put their papers into the box.

'Miss, miss, when are we going to have the questions?', chorused the children. First up was a question from Sam, who wanted to know why, in school assembly, did they ask for the 'Lord's elbow'? Wasn't it only the Catholics who collected old bones?

'Well, what exactly do you say in assembly, Sam?', asked Miss Simms.

'Well, we pray, "Give us thy elbow, Lord".'

Miss Simms smiled as though we kids were about three, gave a little giggle despite herself and shaking her head, explained, 'Oh no, Sam. You see, what you're really saying is, "Give us thy help, O Lord"'.

After that, there were some boring questions from the older girls like, 'Does God mind if we play Postman's Knock?', which Miss Simms rambled on about for ages without saying yes or no. Then there was an amazing one from Jacko who asked why Jesus had such big hands. 'How do you know Jesus had very big hands?', quizzed Miss Simms, looking puzzled.

'Well,' said Jacko confidently, 'at the last supper, didn't six of his disciples sit on his right hand and six on his left?'. Miss Simms coughed and spluttered and the class tittered at the funny picture this made in their minds. Miss Simms clapped her hands and called them to order. Then James (his mother said he hadn't to be called Jimmy) had his question picked out of the box.

'Did Moses really ride a motorbike?' Well, Miss Simms nearly choked. She was the one to go red this time.

'Of course not! Don't be ridiculous, James. How can you say that? Moses lived thousands of years ago before anyone had ever heard of motorbikes!' James wasn't going to be thought an idiot.

'Well, Miss. Why does it say in the bible, "Then the sound of Moses' triumph was heard throughout the land"?' The whole group burst out laughing (well, all the boys anyway). The laughter risked disturbing the service going on through the glass door.

'Now that's enough children. That will do! You're taking the Lord's name in vain. We will have no more questions today.'

And that is how Tom never got to ask his own question and they never got to have a question box again. Tom's mother decided he needn't go to Sunday school anymore, so he joined the cubs instead, which was the beginning of his discovery of the world beyond the street.

It was all of twenty-five years later when all the family were gathered for his mother's funeral service that Tom found himself back in the church at the top of that street. Naturally, it wasn't the same vicar but everything else was so familiar that Tom felt nine years old again, sitting on the side benches with the other kids waiting to be shepherded out of the side door into Sunday school. It was the bit of the gospel where Jesus is exhorting his followers to pay their dues to the Romans. The vicar intoned, 'For Jesus said, "Render unto Caesar, that which is Caesar's"'. Something double-clicked inside him like one of those little metal cricket toys.

'That which is Caesar's…'

'That witch's scissors!'

Tom's son, aged eight, was listening to it all in awe. He turned to his father and whispered, 'What does it all mean, Dad?'.

'You may well ask, son', whispered Tom.

THE HAND THAT FEEDS YOU

I am not going to bite my nails any more.

It's a habit that has held me back in life. At the very least it has stood in the way of my wearing, as is the fashion, a ring on every finger. These long, deadly polished nails announce to the observer that these hands don't work - not manual work at any rate. If you have ever tried gripping a bread-knife, for example, for any length of time with your fingers so adorned, you would know this. Ditto for bread and pastry making. Nothing is more repulsive than picking out bits of dough clogged under the nails. So from now on, those activities are not for me.

Yes, I have always envied those women whose slim, pale digits have known instinctively how to charm. They plane over the sofa arm, dismiss an argument, wafting the air towards you with the back of the hand, offering the added flash of a large diamond ring if the owner is moneyed and over fifty. These fingers let the slackly-fitting rings slip down to the knuckles. Then both hands can be joined together in pushing back the rings, with fingers splayed and stretched in elegant gestures. These women (especially if French) constantly comb their fingers through their hair rakishly, provocatively, all the while seeming to add a dash of exasperation, dismissal or angst to the flow.

I was not given those sorts of hands. Mine are short and square with babyish rounded pads of flesh on each finger between the knuckles and the first joints. On the middle finger of my right hand is a hard lump caused by years of scratching away to pass exams, and just next to that is a paler square of mottled skin where, when I was twelve, I pasted on an Elastoplast soaked in wart-remover that worked only too well. And then again, I had always bitten my nails.

Thanks to my unkempt nails, I couldn't be bothered trying to be glamourous and I suppose that's why I was fated to hang around with Henry at university. I felt comfortable with Henry, he was my sort of man. Henry of the home-knits, unpractical, nerdy Henry. He didn't care about the way he looked, so why should he care about the way I looked as long as I fed him with home-baked cakes and told him how his skills on the computer would earn him a bomb one day.

Unfortunately, his hunger had only been for Anne-Emilie, my flat-mate of the long nails and even longer hair. She once asked me to make her a sandwich as she couldn't slice the bread because of her nails. By the time Anne-Emilie had run off with her fashion design tutor it was too late for me. Henry sublimated his rejection into his new dot com enterprise and turned his back on the outside world and I lost him. When I left university I had no-one. I decided to change my image. There was no way I was going to be a domesticated pudding of a woman.

I started using nail-colour to varnish over the cracks of my self-esteem. My nails gradually grew under their blood-red shroud. I grew my hair a little longer in order to run my fingers through it. I took to cigarettes, to poise in the air, to occupy my lips. *Et me voilà!* No longer sitting gauchely in the passenger seat, clutching my handbag on my lap like my mother used to do. My hands became the outward expression of the personality I longed to have. It became natural to lean into the glove-compartment, take out a cloth and wipe the windscreen for the driver, or riffle through the cassettes and insert something suitable to the mood, or examine a charm bracelet (*de rigueur* to wear this on the same wrist as the watch), or light a cigarette. At a job interview, I actually leaned forward to enumerate the reasons why I should have the job with a tap of each fingernail (French manicure) on the manager's desk. I got the job.

By the time Henry came to visit, after catching up on Facebook, I had got myself nicely installed in my *deux-pièces* in Lyon. My now quite perfect almond-shaped nails had become the antennae and catalysts for the metamorphosis of the whole. Of course, as a result of smoking and coffee only for breakfast, a new slimmer me had emerged. I had begun to dress myself not only on the outside but underneath too, *à la Française*. Functional white underwear could hardly contribute to the *je ne sais quoi* I had cultivated under shorter, tighter skirts. More time is spent pressing clothes to be worn each day, it is true, but then time is saved by not baking cakes or bread. It's an interesting fact that there is no equivalent in French for the verb to bake. And why should there be? Napoleon put paid to home baking by decreeing that every commune had its *boulangerie*. How can home-made cakes hold a candle to the shop's patisseries?

So, by the time Henry came, I was ready for him, nails sharpened. I had been too comfortable for him from the start, mothering him, doing his ironing and baking cakes, so on this reunion I would flick him into touch like the ball in a game of Subbuteo.

We met at the airport and had a coffee in the bar. He was obviously impressed because he kept exclaiming, 'How different you are!'. I left a generous tip so the barman would know I wasn't English. I bought a fresh *ficelle* and patisseries for dessert. At the flat, Henry admired the view of the river from the tiny balcony, the cane chaise-longue, the hammock, and then sat on the edge of the clic clac sofa he would be sleeping on later. 'Crikey, Margaret, you certainly know how to do things!', he mumbled, staring at the table (I had laid it with three tiers of matching plates, candles and two wine glasses at each place, from which blossomed forth two flimsy Japanese-style napkins).

'And about time too', I thought, as he uncorked the wine clumsily. I set it on a pewter wine-tray. 'Really?', I remarked nonchalantly as I erotically fitted the bottle-collar down over its neck and stopped mid-track so that he could see my hands (predatorily blood-red).

He was gaucheness personified. He sat and fiddled with a package he had obviously wrapped himself (shops don't do that for you in England do they?). 'Here,' he said at last, 'I brought these for you. You might as well have them, but somehow I don't think...'. I perched myself next to him, legs crossed and skirt slipping up a little. I smoothed it down slowly with my hands, stroking my thighs.

'Oh you shouldn't have', I giggled as I slid a finger under the sellotaped edge. A pair of sheepskin mittens flopped out onto my lap. 'From Swaledale', he said, staring hard at them, then pleadingly at me. 'I'll have them stuffed and mounted! No really, they're sweet, they really are. They remind me of uni.'

After an aperitif of *kir royal*, I went into the kitchen to put the finishing touches to the dinner. Henry shambled in and wanted to know if he could help. This is strictly not done in France where guests are guests and know their place but I couldn't shake him off somehow. He wanted to know if I still baked bread and cakes. 'Oh that old domesticated me has gone forever!', I shot back. I was preparing a raspberry *coulis* for the patisseries, trying not to get the red juice everywhere and deciding to leave the dishes for the next morning as my nails were really too perfect to risk. 'No really, there was nothing he could do. Have another aperitif? I know, you could cut the *ficelle* and put it into the little silver filigree basket for the table.'

'Where's the bread-knife?', he wanted to know.

'Oh, you don't use a bread-knife, you use the guillotine - there's one on top of the fridge.' Never had Henry been so irritatingly ham-fisted. He grabbed the wooden handle, thinking no doubt it could be lifted like Excalibur from its stone. The whole thing clattered on the tiled floor, narrowly missing my foot. 'Good grief Henry, you never change do you?' He insisted on tackling the guillotine and joked,

'I haven't come over to France to let you do all the work like I used to.' He was a changed man, he said. He had gone through the 'being interested in superficial looks' stage and realised that what mattered was the person inside. Together we lifted the guillotine back onto the fridge.

'Here,' I said more gently, feeling something stir inside as I looked at his earnest face and thought of the sheepskin mitts, 'you grip the handle - hard. My nails dig into my palm if I do it. I'll hold the bread on the base so it won't slip'.

'All those little things you used to do for me. I didn't realise it at the time, but I missed you, you know. I took you for granted. Now I know how much you mean to me. Is it too late? I can see you're changed - maybe you're way out of my league now.' He spoke pleadingly, raising his eyes to mine as he did as I asked.

I was pressing the bread stick confidently down on the base, over the cutting-line, fingers fanned out for his approval. He was looking deeply into my eyes when he shot the blade down quick and hard just like I had told him it should be done.

I won't be biting my nails any more.

THE MOLE-CATCHER

'Do you feel really settled here now, you two?', asked Jim's brother Des, the last of their summer visitors, helping himself to another glass of Medoc. 'I mean, do you think you'll stay here in Normandy?'

'You mean do we want to die here?', Liz threw at him. She paused before answering, 'The truth is, well it's marvellous in summer, eating outside, all this lovely countryside, peace and quiet. The only thing you see on the road is an odd tractor now and then. Only… in the winter it can be a bit lonely, a bit primitive somehow. And of course, whilst it's wonderful to be together so much, well…'. She trailed off and picked at the tablecloth.

'Nonsense,' said Jim, squaring up to the challenge, 'this is where real life is, rediscovering rural skills, enjoying the natural world around us in a simple, unspoiled way. There's always plenty to do in the garden, wood to chop for the fire, everything to keep tidy. It's what I've always wanted, just Elizabeth and me, and a house in the country away from it all'.

'The trouble with that,' Liz murmured, still looking at the tablecloth, 'is that Jim's idea of a country garden is a replica of an English bowling green. He won't see that it's a losing battle'.

'It isn't at all!', snorted Jim, his face reddening, 'You'll not find much moss or weeds out there now, after all the work I've put into that lawn!'.

And it was true. The huge garden was a neat rolling lawn of softly-cropped tender grass, of which their French neighbours were in awe. Only the moles remained a thorn in Jim's flesh. Like an adolescent troubled by acne, Jim would scrutinise the epidermis of his garden every morning from the threshold of the kitchen door and exclaim, 'I knew it! Another one!', and would rush off to scrub away the offending blackhead, scrape away the black puss of soil and camouflage the embarrassing area with green cuttings. The moles became an obsession from which he could not be distracted by murmured praises like the flower-beds, the fruit-trees, the far vista afforded by the land rolling away from the house into the valley peopled by brown and cream-blotched Normandy cows.

Liz sighed. She had watched him try every remedy; mainstream and marginal, preventative and curative, radical and holistic, traditional smoke bombs and gas bombs lit like sparklers and rammed down the holes. These produced satisfying side-effects of smoke spurting from every pore, but they didn't sort out the root problem of the moles underneath. Primitive, but environmentally friendly, were the empty bottles buried in the soil at strategic points to amplify the passing winds and frighten the moles away. These bogeymen were treated with disdain by the hardy moles. And Liz, seeing all from her vantage point of the kitchen sink or the patio, watched Jim grow desperate. He had awakened an ugly streak buried deep inside him. 'I don't care anymore. I could murder them. I want 'em dead. They're spoiling my garden, our life. It's them or me, Liz.'

That day he stomped off first thing, disappeared for hours and came home, triumphant, with poisonous worms, pink, glistening and slimy.

They were artificial, but as soon as Jim snipped open the packet, the smell was just too nauseating for him so he pushed them along the kitchen counter to Liz.

After that, Liz was no longer allowed simply to watch. She was involved, conscripted, persuaded to carry out the operation. 'Isn't it always like this?', she mused. But, as always, she thought she had to. She was taken aback by the tight little cramp she felt deep inside her each time she drew a worm from the envelope, and dropped it into the abyss of the mole tunnel. She gasped for breath and covered her face. Jim sealed the holes with bits of roof-tiles. The roof-tiles caught in the blades of the mower, but the moles lived on to fight another day. 'At least,' muttered Liz to herself, whilst arranging some fine stemmed geraniums in a vase, 'he is not under my feet in the house'. Let him fret over the moles, she thought as she plonked a flower in the vase. Had she not fretted enough over the years? She jammed another flower in even though the vase was tightly packed. Let him bore their visitors and the locals about the moles and give her some peace. She rammed the last geranium in and the water overflowed onto the polished sideboard.

Jim did his research on Google and found the surprising tit-bit of information that moles are in fact, haemophiliacs, in that if they bleed, they die. 'Listen to this Liz! If you push rose-branches or barbed-wire down the galleries, the creatures are bound to puncture themselves and thus die a lingering death!' Liz gasped and gripped the kitchen counter. 'Are you all right, pet?', shouted Jim from his study. He didn't wait for a reply, he was off into the garden without a second thought for Liz. 'All's fair in love and war. Out of sight, out of mind, so to speak', Jim said grimly, as he pushed wires down holes, pleased that the coup de grace would be executed underground, with no dead bodies to be disposed of.

'This of course is why he hasn't put down traps', said Liz to herself, watching him from the front door. 'He could, but that would be to confront death in the face. To recover the trap you have to pull back the spring and look at the awfulness of the small, mangled body. Well, I suppose I shouldn't be surprised that he won't do that.' Liz knew how Jim felt about that. It was the same sensation she had facing trout on the draining board. Until the heads were severed and quickly covered with kitchen paper so that she could handle them, without touching the eyes, she could never continue slicing open the gut and scraping the black blood and greyish insides away from the spine. Thank God for her Marigolds to help her clean away all unacceptable evidence of a palpitating life.

At dinner that particular October evening with Jim's brother, Liz tried to turn the conversation away from moles. 'Did I tell you Monsieur Cauce came to the English lesson with a present this week? He handed me a carrier bag saying he hoped we'd have "une bonne bouffe". Well, when I peeked inside it there was a dead bird - a pheasant he had shot at the weekend in the Sologne. He was so proud of his gift and all I could do was to stare at this thing with all its feathers on, its head twisted to one side to fit in the bag and its claws sticking up pathetically pawing the air. He told me I could put it in the freezer and all I could think was "Where does all the blood go?" and "Who is going to do the dirty work?". He told me in gory detail how to hold it over a gas flame when it was plucked in order to singe the skin and sterilise it. Not to mention how I should save the gizzard after drawing out all the entrails. That's what *salade de gésier* is, you know - gizzard salad.'
'So who did gut the pheasant and clean it up, you or Jim?', asked Des.
'Nobody,' snapped Liz, 'it's like the lawn. We English come here saying we want to live the country life when what we really want is a sort of anglicised, prettified version of it. The French know nature for what it really is - red in tooth and claw'.

The next winter was a long one for Liz. It brought the hunters out - right up to the house, so that she hardly felt safe putting out the washing. She was startled to catch sight of a man with a rifle hidden behind a large, lazy roll of hay just beyond the sunken hedge. Hunters gathered in groups at the corners of country roads looking across the fields and into the woods.

Liz and Jim were walking not far from home one bitter January afternoon when two wild boars thundered down a hillside and crossed the lane not fifty yards in front of them. Their bulky brown bodies bristled and gasped but never deviated from their desperate run from the rifles up on the hill. A pungent stench hovered in the boars' wake. It shocked Liz. It was too much she thought, like the sickly-sweet dark blood and clots of flesh the operating surgeon had provoked all those years ago. It had been the sacrifice Jim had demanded as a condition of marriage. 'What we need is a clean, fresh beginning, time to get to know each other before children come. There will be others', he said. 'We're only in our twenties after all.' Elizabeth had given in, setting the pattern. But there had been no others.

Spring had hardly arrived. Jim was already raking the lawn of the debris of winter, when a voice called at the garden gate. 'Excusez-moi, Monsieur. I'm looking for the Gallets' house.' Jim found himself looking at a short, stocky Norman figure and a wrinkled, venerable face with warm brown eyes. Unprompted, the man told Jim that the Gallets were Parisians and that they had called him about their moles. 'You're a mole-catcher, you say?' Jim's eyes dilated in fascination. Curious at hearing a stranger's voice, Liz appeared at the kitchen door.

'Mais bien sûr monsieur,' the mole-catcher was saying, 'the paysans know quite well how to deal with their moles, but these Parisians can't bear to confront nature, real nature that is. They don't want to dirty their hands'.

'Well now, do you think you could do the same for us, Mr Mole-Catcher?', Jim practically begged. The man told Jim that for forty euros he would lay down special two-pronged, pincer-shaped traps inside the main runs of the moles. He would make good the holes in the lawn when he was satisfied the moles were all caught.

Liz made a special effort for the mole-catcher when he reported back to say the traps were all laid. 'Un croissant et un café-calva, monsieur?' The mole-catcher slowly poured the calvados into the coffee and as he drank he looked at her. She wanted to shrink from his wise and knowing gaze as he took in her beige, tailored trousers and cream linen shirt buttoned up to the collar, just so.

'Vous êtes bien ici, Madame?', he quizzed, turning his head a little but still staring into her soul. Before she could launch into a sociably acceptable response, he pursued, 'Bien dans votre peau?'. She knew this translates as 'good in your skin' but that it really means 'at one with yourself'. As she slowly raised her eyes and found the courage to look into his, she saw twenty-five years of her own repressed emotions which she recognised as pure resentment. 'We must all accept our nature, Madame, and find a way to live with our past', he said softly.

When he had gone, she did not say a word to Jim, but went straight up to the attic. She had been putting this off all her married life. She had not found the courage to delve into the past. It was time to confront her memories in their naked truthfulness. No wonder her resentment had been more intense here in France with no work commitments or family concerns.

When she had pulled herself up amongst the beams and looked round to get her bearings, she headed straight for the darkest corner where, underneath a crumpled blanket, was the wicker Moses basket she had trimmed with voile twenty-five years before and inside it was the snow-white layette she had tenderly collected. When the tears started, they didn't stop. She cried through the night as if twenty-five years of resentment and anger would melt away if only she could cry a river big enough. 'Have you got a cold, pet?', Jim mumbled, the only time her crying woke him. 'You should see what that mole-catcher's done! I'll show you tomorrow. What a difference that's going to make to our garden.'

The next day, before Jim was up, Liz took a stroll round the garden. She lifted her eyes now and then to see the magnificent countryside - a vast bowl of land, thickly wooded along its rim to the North and West, slopes of reddish earth tilled in huge rectangles and bordered by bramble hedges now shrouded with Old Man's Beard. Here and there an orchard, its apple trees hung with mistletoe, sheltered bespectacled cows splashed with the same reddish-brown of the earth. Six little velvety corpses were hung on the barbed wire fence at the entrance to the field. 'Perfect. Bloody perfect, now we've got rid of the moles', she heard Jim say over her shoulder. She had not even noticed he was there. She turned on her heel and went into the house. He went into his shed to fettle his lawnmower.

It took her just two hours to pack up all that she needed. Twenty-five years compressed into two hours. As she drove off, Elizabeth knew Jim would be wondering where she would go, but she knew he would not try to contact her, at least not until the laundry basket was overflowing and the fridge was empty. He would probably have no idea why she had left. And she had no idea why she had not left years ago. Why she had agreed to his monstrous idea of a clean slate before he would marry her.

And as she drove, her favourite music, Vivaldi's Four Seasons, playing defiantly, she wondered what he would think when he went into the kitchen and his eye caught the small cardboard box on the table. Lifting the lid and a piece of cotton wool underneath, he would see a perfect little mole, its paws more like hands and feet - pink and vulnerable, like its upturned nose. She had left it curled up on its side as though it were in the womb.

THE PRESENT CONDITIONAL

If only I had not become curious. I was eight years old when I found it in a huge chest in my mother's bedroom. Of course I couldn't lift it out on my own, so I called down to Mum. 'Ah my little Lucy, so you're old enough for that now are you?', she smiled. 'Well, let me tell you about it.'

As we lifted the dolls' house out of the chest with some difficulty, my mother told me how it had been in the family for generations. Now, the dolls' house really belonged to an aunt and uncle who lived in India. They had left it for me to play with but, as it was so precious and as they were hoping at some point to be blessed with a daughter themselves, they were only entrusting it to me until they came back from India. My mother explained that it was the right time for me to have it since I could now understand the conditions that went along with it. 'Because you mustn't damage or wear it out, you see', said Mum. We carried the dolls' house across the landing into my bedroom and then mum went down to carry on with the vacuuming.

Set atop the only table in my room, it was just at my eye-level and I was immediately struck by its splendour. It was half-timbered like one of those old Elizabethan houses in my history book. In all there were nine windows - two at either side of the front porch downstairs and five upstairs. On the imposing front door above the brass knocker there was the name Nirvana. In the upstairs rooms there were four-poster beds with curtains around and rectangles of carpet with an armchair or a dressing-table on them. Downstairs, I could see a dining-room with a table and eight chairs, a parlour with a picture over the fireplace and two old-fashioned sofas. The best room though was the kitchen where there was no carpet - just a white-painted wooden floor. On the back wall of the kitchen was a tall dresser with tiny plates and dishes painted blue and white, propped up on the shelves at the top. On the square table in the middle was a rubber chicken or perhaps a turkey (it was so big) all trussed up and ready to go into the big black stove that had a chimney reaching up to the ceiling.

Naturally, I was fascinated by my new toy and soon could remember every detail of it, which I used to recite to my mother on journeys to town. 'Next to the kitchen stove are some cloth pads on a hook. I think they are to stop your hands burning when you take something out of the stove.'

'I'm sure you're right, Lucy.'

'Do you think it's a turkey or only a chicken on the kitchen table, Mum?'

'It's whatever you want it to be, dear.'

It was a shame that my dolls were all too big to fit in the house. I couldn't reach inside the doors or the windows because they didn't open. In order to get inside, you had to take the whole front of the house off - porch and all. The front was fastened on by a series of hooks and catches. Mum said not to try as I might break something. So I left the many rooms undisturbed and spent many an hour admiring it, pondering its every detail without touching anything inside. It was a bit like a birthday cake so beautifully decorated that no-one wants to cut through the icing to taste the cake.

Except once, that is. It was when I was eleven and a new girl at the big school. It seemed to me that all the other girls were important in some way that I wasn't. In what way each girl was important might differ. It might be two names announced to a new teacher instead of one, like Anne-Marie or Hilary-Ann. Or the fact that a girl carried an old leather satchel which was casually observed to have been grandmama's. I had no such pretensions, living in a two-up, two-down terraced house. It was nothing more than a desire to be noticed that prompted me to unhook the facade of my dolls' house and look for something with which to impress my school friends. Much later in life, I realised I should have taken at least something more impressive like the picture from over the fireplace or the china bowl from the table but guilt shot like adrenalin through my veins, activated by a noise on the stairs. I snatched a chair from the miniature dining-room and pushed the facade back against the house. The footsteps went off into another bedroom but the fright I got gave birth to a shot of guilt every time I ever took off the front of the house.

At school, I uncurled my palm to show the little wooden chair to the others amid polite murmurings of 'oh', 'how quaint' and 'did your father make it?'. This anti-climax rapidly induced disappointment which descended into more guilt and misery when, after replacing the chair in the dolls' house, I broke two of the catches trying to hook the facade back into place. Broken! I had broken the house entrusted to me.

After two weeks of purgatory agonising that someone would notice the broken facade and wondering what the aunt and uncle would say when they returned to claim their heirloom, I decided to find out when that day might arrive. 'When are Aunt and Uncle coming back from India, Mum?'

'Sorry dear? What? Oh, well it's going to be a long time off yet dear, because there is so much for them to do, you know, helping the poor people out there.' This was no comfort at all. On the contrary, it only served to make me feel worse. I was off the hook for a good while which should have been a reprieve but that nagging feeling of guilt was compounded now that I knew that some saintly aunt and uncle were dedicating their lives to helping the poor in India. I was obviously not worthy of their generosity.

Since the house was in such a prominent position in my bedroom - necessarily so, because it was too big to fit into a cupboard, and too tall to go under my bed, as the years passed, it became a sort of shrine. I often dreamt of it - or rather the life-sized house it represented and so it made me feel less than satisfied with my humble but real home. Oh, the rapture of imagining myself, wandering through those elegant rooms, straightening the picture over the drawing-room fireplace or placing the blue and white dishes on the kitchen dresser. At such times I became so totally immersed in the scene that I could smell the potpourri in the china bowls and the polish on the furniture. To be on the other side of that facade with the sun streaming right in on me in my own perfect home, must be heaven.

I vowed I would grow up and live in my dolls' house, a real-life version of it, and I would live happily ever after. Yet to be completely happy in the future, you couldn't harbour nasty little secrets in the present like the broken fastenings on the house. I decided to tell all to my mother. After all, that incident had happened quite some time ago when I was only a child. My mother seemed to understand. 'I think you will feel a lot better Lucy, if you write a letter saying what happened and how sorry you are.' I had the fleeting thought that if someone else had broken two catches the size of sixpence on a toy of mine, I wouldn't think twice about it. Still, I wanted everything cleared up so that the dream of my perfect home would remain intact. So I wrote the letter and even managed two pages which was no mean feat since I knew nothing about the people I was writing to.

The dolls' house was the first thing that came into view as I struggled to wake up at my mother's morning call on schooldays. Even as I glanced up from time to time from my homework, sitting on my bed against the metal bedhead, it was there just beyond the foot of the bed, taking up the table and my stories by giving me a framework for them and a doorway into a perfect world. Nonetheless, the worldly preoccupations of teenage girls inhabited my thoughts too. I, like all teenage girls, was learning how to dress to emphasize my prettiness and soon I was standing with the other girls at the edge of the dancefloor, waiting to be asked - and waiting.

Never mind, I pocketed a respectable 2:1 at university as a result of all the waiting for more exciting things to happen apart from studying. Along with a group of friends, I bought rail tickets and spent the next year practising the languages we had learnt until the railway tracks carried us beyond the foreign to the extremely exotic. Here, experiencing the simplest of living styles, I stayed amongst a nomadic people whose possessions were few, since everything must travel with them from place to place. I observed that a guest who admires a possession is pressed to accept it as a gift, unconditionally and forever. I could not be careless, as we westerners are with our little hypocritical compliments, as I could not have born the thought of depriving these people who gave so freely when they had so little.

One night, in Outer Mongolia, in the round tent they call a yurt, and after a feast of cheese, yoghurt and fermented mares' milk, I dreamed of living in my dolls' house. Once again, I was the chatelaine with the keys. Every detail was magnified, so that, as I swished from room to room, adjusting minor perfections, the little dining-room chair that had fitted into my palm was now quite heavy to push under the table. The picture over the fireplace lurched as I straightened it and the blue and white dishes on the kitchen dresser threatened to unbalance and fall to the floor. Strangely, the house keys I carried at my waist gradually became heavier. The house was empty of people and a great loneliness overwhelmed me. I woke in the yurt, hot and troubled. Outside, under the crisp stars, my breathing became calmer as I realised that the perfect life inside the perfect house was not something I wanted any more.

At the end of the year, I came home. My mother was never one to clear out for no good reason and my bedroom was exactly as it had been in my childhood. The dolls' house was still there of course but it looked, well, frankly, it looked shabby. Where was the air of impeccable grandeur, the receptacle of all those dreams of a perfect future? The half-timbering, I could see now, was only painted on, the porch was made of cardboard leaning at a slight angle and the brass-coloured coating on the door-knocker was peeling badly. 'What a sham!', I thought and surprised myself by feeling no guilt whatsoever at thinking so. In fact the whole idea of a house that you can't get into unless you take it to pieces appeared faintly ludicrous. 'Mum,' I said pensively over the tinned pink salmon and salad cream sandwiches, 'whatever happened to Aunt and Uncle, the ones in India helping the poor? Didn't they have any children of their own? Did they ever come back again? Did they forget they'd left me the dolls' house?'. My mother looked totally perplexed, then, suddenly remembering, smiled and told me the truth.

'Oh Lucy! There never was an uncle or an aunt - not really. I just told you that so that you'd look after the dolls' house properly. I got it at the church jumble sale. I always wanted one when I was little but I wasn't as lucky as you.' The soft white bread suddenly stuck in my throat as my mother continued, 'You see, this way, it's in such good condition, you can give it to your own daughter when the time comes. That's what I call an heirloom'.

THE SIMPLE LIFE

The thatched, half-timbered cottage they had bought was charming and the friends who had visited in the summer had been full of admiration for its old, red-tiled floors and quirky heating system. Donald and Jean had presided over drinks and barbecues in the garden with friends who were envious of their simple country lifestyle, far from the madding crowds of England.

'I wonder what that old lady's picking at the side of the road', remarked Jean, gazing through the window one quiet afternoon.
'Her nose?', smirked Donald. Ignoring his sarcasm, Jean walked across the garden to the hedge where she could see the old woman putting dandelion leaves in her basket.
'Bonjour Madame', said Jean.
'Bonjour Madame', replied the old woman. 'Ça fera une bonne petite salade, ces pisses en lits.' Jean giggled, remembering how the class had laughed at the idea of calling a dandelion a 'piss-in-bed'.

'That's what we should do,' said Donald later, when Jean told him about her encounter, 'live off the land, be self-sufficient, save on the supermarket bills and be healthier'. So Jean made a start by picking as many dandelion leaves as she could find in a two-hour walk along the lanes and in fact, in a salad, they tasted a bit like rocket - tangy but tasty, mixed in with lettuce leaves.

Things were not quite so enviable as the winter dragged on. Friends and family stopped coming and Jean sorely missed Christmas in England as Donald felt it was too early to go running back. Her daily routine began to consist of some gardening in the morning, a nap after lunch, a little necessary domestic work and then watching television. 'We might as well be in England,' thought Jean, 'at least the telly is better there'.

Down-sizing to one car seemed sensible. She had been relieved to let Donald drive at first. She'd been nervous and taken the easy way out and anyway, she hadn't anywhere to go on her own. She insisted on driving once or twice, but when she did, Donald couldn't seem to stop himself giving instructions like 'you can overtake now... get into the left-hand lane... change down or you'll never get past'. She didn't drive at all now and Donald referred to it as *his* car.

Of course the garden gave her great pleasure. She would raise her head from her vegetable plot and marvel at the vista of farms, apple orchards, brown and white cows and graceful racehorses below an unending sky. There were moments of delight when sampling her chutney made from the apples that fell from their own trees, or when they sat under a parasol watching the ducks gaggle on the little pond. The eggs from their hens made the lightest omelettes ever. 'Aren't we lucky?', Donald boasted, over their aperitif in the garden.

Quite soon after they had settled in, the old farmer from down the lane started coming round and joining them for a calvados. 'Ça va?', he would ask.

'Ça va.' Donald would raise his glass, leaving Jean wondering at the ease with which he was going native.

The warming spring beckoned Jean out of doors to walk the paths surrounding their cottage. She saw the old lady out gathering young and tender nettles. 'Potage', she said, 'de la soupe!'. So Jean followed suit and gathered nettles. The soup they made was quite good when she stirred cream into it.

She really looked forward to market day in town. Their eyes fell upon the cornucopia of produce on the stalls - dead or alive. 'Gosh! Look at the choice of mushrooms!', exclaimed Jean. 'Let's try some of those for a change?'
'They're too expensive', said Donald. 'Surely we can grow some?' So Jean didn't get to buy any mushrooms from the market. She never had any money on her anyway.

Deeper into autumn there were fat sloes on blackthorn bushes that she could soak in gin, blackberries for pies and rose-hips to make syrup. She really enjoyed doing this whilst Donald took to going with the old farmer to the village café in the early evening before supper. It became part of his routine to spend an hour or two there. 'Only men go to the bars over here Jean. You wouldn't like it.'

The old lady was out again, this time looking for snails. Donald would never eat snails, Jean thought. Later on though, she saw the old lady grubbing for mushrooms in a wooded dell. Jean plucked up the courage to ask. 'C'est bon - les champignons?'
'Oui, très bon. Mais faites attention', and she showed Jean how to pick the mushrooms without damaging them. Donald was pleased with Jean's resourcefulness. She served them in omelettes, casseroles and salads.
'Mm. This is good', Donald remarked about her mushroom soup.

One evening they were invited to a fête in the village hall. Unusually, Donald wasn't against going, in fact was all for it, so Jean put on a simple frock and rooted round for the remnants of her make-up. 'You don't need that all that muck, pet. I like you just as you are. Just be your natural self.'

Once they got there, Jean was surprised at Donald's new-found sociability until she realised his pals from the café were all there and he had people to talk to that he knew. But when she came back from the buffet and saw him dancing to the accordion band she nearly dropped her *pâté en croute*. There he was, shaking it all about with a woman in red high-heels and lipstick to match, who kept flicking her long hair back even when she didn't need to. Jean felt her stomach turn over and over with anger and humiliation. She felt as if she'd been somehow cheated. Donald had the good life all right and she was left out. She felt discarded. The resentment built and anger surged. 'I do all the domestic work and make the meals, and now I'm doing the gardening and growing lots of vegetables too. He still has a social life just as he had in England. He still has a wife who washes and irons his clothes and makes his meals', she muttered to herself. 'He still has his own car, for God's sake!'

When the dance finished she went over and demanded to go home. 'Oh don't be so silly, pet. You're not jealous are you? Claudine is Jean-Paul's wife and it would be impolite not to dance with her.' Everything that had happened in the last year boiled over in Jean's stomach. She excused herself, saying she needed to go to the lavatory. She decided to leave and walk home alone - bitter bile rising in her throat. Just who exactly, was leading the simple life?

She had been tossing restlessly for at least two hours when there was a knock at the door and two policemen were standing there. 'Votre mari est à l'hôpital Madame', said one of them. 'C'est peut-être grave.'

'Un accident?', whispered Jean.

'Non, non, il est tombé malade à la fête.'

'Oh my God, I hope he's all right', fretted Jean in the police car. The bitterness she had felt earlier turned into guilt.

Donald was pale and sweating and in quite some pain when she arrived. She looked anxiously at the nurses. 'Trop de Calvados?', she asked. The nurses assured her it wasn't drink. So what was it then? Jean agonised. She stayed the rest of the night but she couldn't help the doctors at all with their diagnosis. By morning, Donald was asleep and the situation was on hold, so the nurse insisted, 'Retournez à la maison et dormez'. She got a taxi to the village, picked up the car and drove it home.

In no time at all she fell asleep and slept late. It was about two o'clock in the afternoon when she was preparing to leave for the hospital when someone knocked on the door. It was the old woman with a young girl who spoke in broken English. 'Madame, my grandmother is not happy. The champignons you get are maybe not good. Maybe very bad. Vénéneux. You must not eat.' Jean closed the door and sank into Donald's armchair.

'Had she given Donald poisonous mushrooms?', she thought. 'Oh my God! Was it possible? Could Donald really die from the mushrooms she had picked and cooked for him?' She couldn't think sensibly. Of course the mushrooms couldn't have been poisonous, she had eaten them too! But she couldn't stop her mind wandering to a dreadful scenario. What would she do if Donald died? Panic? Yes! Be devastated? Er… yes. But what would she do? Well, she would have to contact the family of course. But what would Donald want? Would he want to be taken back to England? Would he want to be buried or cremated? What sort of service would he like? He wasn't really religious but when pressed, he would mention his mother's favourite hymn 'The Day Thou Gavest Lord is Ended'.

She got up to make herself a cup of tea, hoping to break this dreadful train of thought. But she couldn't stop herself thinking how nice it was being able to make a cup of tea without anybody saying, 'I'm ready for a coffee whilst you're up, Jean'. She had to pull herself together. After all, she had driven the car home unaided and yet she had not crashed it. After a nice cup of tea she began to think she might be able to cope with life after all.

Jean let the sun invite her into the garden. She greeted the chickens, looked lovingly at the strawberries spreading and flowering and the rhubarb reaching up like umbrellas above them. Thinking of the poisonous mushrooms reminded her that lots of plants are dangerous to eat - rhubarb stems are great in puddings and in jam, but eat the leaves and you will be sick indeed. Even the yew tree leaves, looking so like rosemary, are apparently deadly to humans. The phone ringing through the open kitchen window jolted her out of her reverie. 'It's me, pet. I'm feeling a lot better now. The doc says there's nothing serious but they'll do some tests and then I can come home. If you set off now, I'll be ready when you arrive. Now, take the handbrake off before you move and don't grind those gears.'

THERE'S NO PLACE LIKE HOME

Everybody said they would blow down just like the little pigs' house did - the one made of straw. We didn't care. We were going to have a brand-new house, all to ourselves. We had been living with Tom's mum in her two-up, two-down for most of the war. We already had Sam and I was pregnant again. It was a dream come true.

We went to have a look before we moved in. What a shock it was to see so many houses - more than forty, on the farmer's field where Tom used to go ferreting. Little Sam's eyes popped out when he saw a house swing in the air! A whole house, four walls, a door and four windows with some kind of flat roof dangling from a crane! The fellows working there told us they were putting them up within two days apiece. Made of tin mostly, they were. I must say we went back to Tom's mother's a bit let down at the thought of living in a tin house. But the night before we moved in, I couldn't sleep for excitement.

There were two bedrooms - both bigger than at Tom's mum's, and a bathroom. Just imagine - a bathroom! With a bath and a washbasin and a toilet next door to it that you could use if somebody was using the bathroom. Wasn't that thoughtful? Nobody on our old street had a bathroom - just a tin bath filled from the copper and a long-drop lavatory out the back. Having hot water on tap was going to be heaven.

The living-room was light and airy and had a closed-in fire with a door which meant you could keep it in all night if you wanted. What a cosy room it was! Tom's mum bought me a set of ducks that Tom put up on the wall over the fireplace as though they were flying towards the window and the hills beyond. How we saved to make that room nice! We got a leatherette three-piece suite on the never-never and bought a radiogram to listen to of an evening.

My mum spent six months making a rag rug to put down in front of the fire. No sooner had we put that rug down than Tom managed to burn a hole in it, riddling the fire too energetically. He would do that, no matter if the children were still sleeping - he said it got the whole house moving of a morning! One morning he did that all right, he chipped a couple of tiles with the poker. Try as I did to cover the hole in the rug with a triangle of cut cloth, my eye always went straight to it the minute I sat down.

The kitchen was the best room of all - my palace, my kingdom. It had a built-in kitchenette, a cupboard with a drop-down ironing-board and an electric cooker and washing-machine, all ready for us. The kitchen was so big we could eat in it. In fact we only ate in the living-room when we had a family do, like at Christmas.

Our pre-fab might well have been made of tin but it was very special tin. Not many people know that war-damaged aircraft were melted down to make the tin sheets they were built of and that prisoners of war helped to produce them. When people moved in after the war, they had running water and electric appliances for the first time in their lives. Nobody we knew in the old terraced rows had a house like mine inside, and a garden too, not just a backyard. Tom remembered his old uncle who'd had an allotment and he took to growing our vegetables. We had lovely cabbage, leeks, rhubarb and fruit bushes. He even planted an apple tree. My sisters and brothers came with their families and my apple pies were much appreciated.

When Jenny was three and Sam was seven, Tom divided the second bedroom in two. It was clever the way he did it, putting glass in the top of the partition wall to let the light through. We managed that way until the children left home.

Television came along in time for the Queen's coronation and we invited our friends in to watch. Those who lived in the streets and who hadn't seen inside our prefab were really surprised at how spacious and modern it was. I showed them the kitchen and the bathroom with pride. Me, I loved this house - the way it had cupboards tucked into every recess so you have a place for everything and everything in its place.

To think these prefabs were only supposed to be a temporary solution to the housing shortage after the war! Fifteen years they were supposed to last and here we were still, almost thirty years later. Since those early days, we haven't done much to the house. We hadn't felt the need to. The kids played in the garden and when they were older, explored the countryside over the fence. Of course, I had to take a bus into town but it was only a five minutes' walk to the bus stop. The kids walked to school until Sam went to secondary school and Jenny later got into the grammar school.

Now that's when things changed. Whereas Sam would invite a friend home to play sometimes, Jenny never did. She always went to someone else's house. When I tackled her about it, she said other peoples' houses were more interesting, but I knew there was more to it than that. We were renting, just like any other council house tenants and I suspect she had begun to compare us with other families - what we had and what others had, what their fathers did compared with her dad, who went to work in overalls. She once said the flying ducks over the mantelpiece were typical CHT. When her dad asked her what on earth that meant, she said, 'Council house taste'. He threw a wobbler at that.

Sam is more like his dad and was content at home. He always liked coming back. The only criticism he ever had was last year when he said it was time I took the antimacassars off the backs of the sofa and armchairs. 'It is 1979 after all!', he said.

Jenny was a bright girl and we were so proud when she got a place at university up in Durham, but, sadly, she grew apart from us. She did bring her young man home before she got engaged and he had the decency to ask Tom for her hand but they went off to live in the South. These last two years have been a big worry to us with her getting divorced. I don't really understand it. He always seemed a mild-mannered sort of chap - not one to give her any trouble. Anyway, she seems all right now. She's a teacher so she won't want for money. She's talking about going to work abroad... so I don't know.

The council have been sending questionnaires round to ask how we would feel about moving. Most people think prefabs are, 'past their sell-by date', as they say nowadays. I don't agree at all but I know people want more and more these days and younger people are turning their noses up at the idea of a prefab. They're all for flats these days. Convenient, they say they are. Claustrophobic I say! Even Sam is beginning to think we should move. He thinks, the way things are going, they'll move us out anyway, sooner or later. So why not have a flat nearer the town centre if they offer one? I'll be sorry to go, though.

———————<<<<———————

I couldn't believe it! Mum and Dad's old prefab was still there! I remember them saying, 'Oh Jenny, you don't realise what a perfect little home this is'. How right they were! Although truth to say, it looked almost too new. They'd put a proper stone wall on the outside and angled the roof a bit to take solar panels. Apparently now it has 'excellent insulation properties' and uses 'alternative energy systems'. That'll be the solar panels and the wind turbine at the top of the garden. Together they provide all the heating, electricity and hot water I'll need. I just love the original kitchenette and the tall cupboard with the drop-down ironing board. With a good coat of paint, the house will look great. I was stripping wallpaper off the other day and came across three dark patches on the bottom layer of paper over the fireplace. What memories it all brings back! I got a man in to take down the partition in the second bedroom, sorry, guest bedroom, where I'll have my computer and my books.

I've worked in South Africa, the USA and even China these last twenty years, but when I retired last year I realised that home was still here in this ordinary northern town. I relish the ready humour of the people here. I'd forgotten just how quick they are off the mark with their jokes - whether it's at your expense or their own it doesn't seem to matter. I wonder what my mother would have to say about it all. I do remember with a tinge of shame that I used to be a bit snotty about our house when I was a teenager. That's when materialistic things seemed to matter. Believe me, when you've seen the most abject poverty in far-flung parts of the world, you realise how lucky we all are in the West - even the poorest of us. I shall be very happy in my little house.

I've already had a house-warming party. Last week I invited everyone who is still living - even the school pals I tracked down through Friends Reunited on the internet. It was fantastic! I laid the buffet out on the kitchen table and played sixties CDs of groups like The Beatles, The Stones and The Eagles non-stop. We were all past the phase of looking each other up and down to see which one of us has done best in life. It was quite clear we all treasure our health (those of us who still have it) and most of us agreed we wanted to seize the day and do everything we can, whilst we can. It still didn't stop us giggling over the memory of Patricia's greasy hair or Jane simpering up to the Latin teacher just because he was a man. We are going to meet up every year from now on. We appreciate that we will be a diminishing number perhaps, from now on, just like the prefabs themselves, but we want to re-live every nostalgic moment.

My prefab is called an eco-house now because it's environmentally correct and even has a compost pit dug in the garden. The blurb the council gave when they sold it to me says it will, 'leave the lightest carbon footprint any habitation can'. I shall grow herbs and all sorts of newly-discovered salads. I'll enjoy using Mum's old recipes and adding herbs and spices she'd never heard of. In the garden I can hear my Dad's voice still. The apple tree he planted is still here. It will be so easy to furnish with a pine table and chairs in the kitchen and a must-have leather Art Deco sofa with a scatter rug on the wooden floor. I'll have a plasma screen over the fireplace but I'll keep the fireplace as it is if I can find some tiles in a reclamation yard to repair a bit of the damage. I might even look round the car-boot sales for some plaster ducks to hang on the wall.

My daughter has flown over from Michigan with her family to help me move in and she thinks my eco-house is adorable. Of course, kit houses, ready to build yourself, are all the rage in Michigan. Here, in my home town, there are just six of the original prefabs left now and each one has a plaque declaring it to be a 'listed conservation property of which the town is proud'.

ABOUT THE AUTHOR

Vivienne Barker was brought up in the Lancashire mill town of Burnley where she had the good fortune to attend a convent grammar school in nearby Oswaldtwistle. She left at 15 to start earning her living and had several years working in a factory office and the civil service before having a son and a daughter. As it was not allowable to work part-time in the civil service, she found a part-time job in a school office, which led her to aspire to being a teacher. After gaining a B.Ed. degree, she began teaching French in secondary comprehensive schools.

In 1991, she and her husband moved to Normandy in France for 15 years culminating in her first book *Comme Ci, Comme Ça* (available at *www.amazon.co.uk*) examining amusing and annoying differences between the British and the French cultures.

Vivienne now resides back in the United Kingdom in the gorgeous county of Shropshire. The first years of her retirement were spent collating and revising her short stories inspired by people-watching during the second half of the 20th and into the 21st century.

Printed in Great Britain
by Amazon